"If you're ever in a bind, give me a shout. I may not be much help, though."

Katorina

One of the main heroines present on the *Magical★Explorer* box art. A competitive spirit who is sensitive about her meager bust.

"So you don't think anything about me right now?"

Stef

Serves as the captain of the Morals Committee. The Acting Saint from Leggenze. Although she is beautiful, compassionate, and popular with the students...is there more to her than meets the eye...?

Anemone

A dark elf and genius inventor from the Trèfle Empire who serves as the magistrate of the Ceremonial Committee. People say she's a pervert, and she's inclined to agree.

"I've been waiting for you. Oh, but I hate my surname, so Anemone's fine."

Gabby

Ceremonial Minister Benito Evangelista's younger sister. A beautiful honors student who is haughty and competitive. Also has a kind side.

"Unh…unghh…"

Magical★Explorer

Reborn as a Side Character in a Fantasy Dating Sim

—Volume 5

Iris

ILLUSTRATION BY
Noboru Kannatuki

YEN ON
New York

Magical★Explorer: Reborn as a Side Character in a Fantasy Dating Sim, Vol. 5

Iris

Translation by David Musto
Cover art by Noboru Kannatuki

This book is a work of fiction. Names, characters, places, and incidents are the product of the author's imagination or are used fictitiously. Any resemblance to actual events, locales, or persons, living or dead, is coincidental.

MAGICAL★EXPLORER ERO GAME NO YUJIN KYARA NI TENSEI SHITAKEDO, GAME CHISHIKI TSUKATTE JIYUNI IKIRU Vol. 5
©Iris, Noboru Kannatuki 2021
First published in Japan in 2021 by KADOKAWA CORPORATION, Tokyo.
English translation rights arranged with KADOKAWA CORPORATION, Tokyo through TUTTLE-MORI AGENCY, INC., Tokyo.

English translation © 2023 by Yen Press, LLC

Yen Press, LLC supports the right to free expression and the value of copyright. The purpose of copyright is to encourage writers and artists to produce the creative works that enrich our culture.

The scanning, uploading, and distribution of this book without permission is a theft of the author's intellectual property. If you would like permission to use material from the book (other than for review purposes), please contact the publisher. Thank you for your support of the author's rights.

Yen On
150 West 30th Street, 19th Floor
New York, NY 10001

Visit us at yenpress.com ★ facebook.com/yenpress ★ twitter.com/yenpress ★ yenpress.tumblr.com ★ instagram.com/yenpress

First Yen On Edition: July 2023
Edited by Yen On Editorial: Maya Deutsch
Designed by Yen Press Design: Andy Swist

Yen On is an imprint of Yen Press, LLC.
The Yen On name and logo are trademarks of Yen Press, LLC.

The publisher is not responsible for websites (or their content) that are not owned by the publisher.

Library of Congress Cataloging-in-Publication Data
Names: Iris (Light novel author), author. | Kannatuki, Noboru, illustrator. | Musto, David, translator.
Title: Magical explorer / Iris ; illustration by Noboru Kannatuki ; translation by David Musto.
Other titles: Magical explorer. English
Description: First Yen On edition. | New York, NY : Yen On, 2021–
Identifiers: LCCN 2021039072 | ISBN 9781975325619 (v. 1 ; trade paperback) | | ISBN 9781975325633 (v. 2 ; trade paperback) | ISBN 9781975325657 (v. 3 ; trade paperback) | ISBN 9781975350482 (v. 4 ; trade paperback) | ISBN 9781975350512 (v. 5 ; trade paperback)
Subjects: CYAC: Video games—Fiction. | Role playing—Fiction. | Magic—Fiction. | Fantasy. | LCGFT: Light novels.
Classification: LCC PZ7.1.I76 Mag 2021 | DDC [Fic]—dc23
LC record available at https://lccn.loc.gov/2021039072

ISBNs: 978-1-9753-5051-2 (paperback)
        978-1-9753-5052-9 (ebook)

10 9 8 7 6 5 4 3 2 1

LSC-C

Printed in the United States of America

Chapter Select

Magical★Explorer

CONTENTS

Illustration: Noboru Kannatuki

Graphic Design: Kai Sugiyama (Tsuyoshi Kusano Design Co., Ltd.)

Characters

Kousuke Takioto

The best friend character from *Magical ★ Explorer*. The soul of a Japanese eroge aficionado dwells within him. Possesses a unique ability.

Ludie

Ludivine Marie-Ange de la Tréfle.

Highborn second daughter to the emperor of the elven Tréfle Empire. A main heroine who appears on the game packaging for *Magical ★ Explorer*.

Nanami

A maid created to assist Dungeon Masters. Belongs to the angel race, who are few in number.

Marino Hanamura

Principal of Tsukuyomi Magic Academy, the game's main setting. Receives limited screen time in the game, so she's shrouded in mystery.

Hatsumi Hanamura

Marino Hanamura's daughter and Kousuke's second cousin. Generally very quiet and reserved. Teaches at Tsukuyomi Magic Academy.

Claris

Elf who serves as Ludie's bodyguard and maid. Serious and devoted to her mistress, she has a tendency to beat herself up over her failures.

Iori Hijiri

The main character in the game version of *Magical ★ Explorer*. Ordinary in appearance. When developed, however, he becomes the strongest character in the game.

Yuika Hijiri

Iori Hijiri's younger stepsister. A main heroine who is featured on the game's box art. Transferred to Tsukuyomi Magic Academy.

Rina Katou

Katorina.

One of the main heroines present on the *Magical ★ Explorer* box art. A competitive spirit who is sensitive about her meager bust.

Monica

Monica Mercedes von Mobius.

The president of the Student Council. One of *Magical ★ Explorer's* Big Three and a main heroine who features on the game's packaging.

Stef

Stefania Scaglione.

Serves as the captain of the Morals Committee. The Acting Saint from Leggenze. Although she is beautiful, compassionate, and popular with the students… is there more to her than meets the eye…?

Benito

Benito Evangelista.

Serves as the ceremonial minister, the president of the Ceremonial Committee. Despised by the students of the Academy, but beloved by eroge players.

Fran

Franziska Edda von Gneisenau.

Serves as vice president of the Student Council. An extremely earnest and diligent girl. Sees Yukine and Shion as her rivals.

Yukine Mizumori

One of the officially recognized overpowered characters who are collectively referred to as the Big Three of *Magical ★ Explorer*. Lieutenant of the Morals Committee.

Shion Himemiya

Serves as ceremonial vice minister of the Ceremonial Committee. Always clad in a kimono instead of her uniform. Her strength is on par with the other main heroines'.

Ivy

Head of the *Tsukuyomi Academy Newspaper*. A rabbitfolk girl

Ms. Ruija

Instructor at Tsukuyomi Magic Academy. Loose with money and

Rue Sakura

Tsukuyomi Academy's librarian. Has cared for many students over

—*Gabriella's Perspective*—

"I absolutely can*not, will* not believe it! Why, the mere thought of it is maddening... *Gaaaaaaah!*"

"Well, I do spend my time trying to make everyone hate me, you know."

"Dear Brother! Be that as it may, what Yuika Hijiri has done is utterly unacceptable!"

I felt annoyed just remembering it. Speaking about me like that was one thing, but to drag Brother into this!

"Come now, Gabriella. Calm down. Those are some awfully strange and unladylike sounds coming from your mouth."

"Do you not think anything of her insults to you?!"

I recalled her teasing voice.

"'That weakling, beans-for-brains ceremonial minister should hurry up and cede his seat to Takioto instead!' And that Kousuke Takioto fellow didn't even *try* to rebut what she was saying."

"Ha-ha-ha... I'm not sure she would say something quite as nasty as that. Could you be dramatizing things a bit?"

"Not in the slightest!"

Admittedly, my memory was a little hazy, but this was the *exact* nuance she'd intended!

"R-really? I expected you to go after Takioto, but Yuika is a surprise..."

"Wh-what did you say just now, dear Brother?! Honestly, my blood boils every time I think back to the insults she spewed. Have you set the stage for our battle like I asked?!"

"Yup, that's moving along. I've found the perfect dungeon for it."

"I hope you also remember your promise."

"Yeah, I do. If you win, then I recommend you join the Ceremonial Committee, right?"

"Yes, that's correct."

"But are you truly prepared to join us? Have you really taken another look at yourself?"

"Of course I've already done that. I want to become the ceremonial minister just like you!"

"Well, as far as that goes, it's already pretty much set in stone that Takioto will take over after me."

"Again with that boy…"

That brute Takioto was ingratiating himself with Brother to manipulate him. I wasn't going to let him use my dear brother as a stepping stone. I needed to stop it from happening.

"What about the Student Council? With your grades as high as they are, they must be talking to you," Brother said.

"I had it in my mind to turn them down tomorrow. More importantly, back to the Ceremonial Committee. There's still a chance I could become ceremonial minister if I do great things in the organization, yes?"

Brother sighed and gave me an exasperated smile.

"Gabriella…"

"Am I not allowed to follow in your footsteps?!"

"No, that's not what I'm getting at. The truth is…I want to see you spread your wings."

"What do you mean? If you're saying you want me to land a prestigious position, why then, I'll aim to be ceremonial minister! I'd say that's spreading my wings out plenty wide, no?"

"That's fair, I suppose."

Could it be?

"Dear Brother, do you have it in your head that Kousuke Takioto is the perfect fit for ceremonial minister?"

Instead of me.

"I do think Takioto will be able to accomplish more in the role than I have," he said.

Again with that boy! Brother was far too trusting of Kousuke Takioto. This was why he was being manipulated.

That settled it—I needed to tear Brother away from Takioto.

"I'm going to bring Kousuke Takioto down."

"What're you talking about?"

"Should I win our upcoming contest, I shall have Kousuke Takioto resign from his position as assistant vice-minister of the Ceremonial Committee."

"There's no way Takioto will agree to that. But let's say you do make some kind of wager—you'll need to offer up something that's just as valuable, too, you know."

"Then I'll bet my enrollment at the Academy. My victory is guaranteed regardless."

Brother mulled over the proposition. However, ultimately...

"If that's enough to make Takioto take you up on your challenge, it's fine by me. I'll leave you two to sort this out."

...he replied with a smile.

"...Please continue with the preparations, dear Brother. I'm going to triumph over Kousuke Takioto and prove that I'm a perfect fit for the Ceremonial Committee!"

I left the living room. As I briskly walked to my room, I released my anger in a deep sigh. Then I collapsed on my back into bed.

"Brother is unparalleled..."

He'd even earned Father's recognition. There couldn't possibly be anyone better than him.

I stretched my hand up toward the ceiling.

As I stared at it, my mind suddenly wandered to the past, back to when I was about to turn ten.

It happened when I'd flopped onto the lawn after having trouble practicing magic. I'd stretched my hand up to the sky the same way I was now...

"Why...why is it so hard?" I'd muttered as I looked at my hand wreathed in mana.

This same exercise had come effortlessly to my brother. Father, Mother, and even the maid all said so. The fact that it was beyond me must have meant that I lacked talent. The mana began to disperse from my hand.

"What're you doing lying around in the grass like that?"

Just then, someone called out to me.

My brother had come over to me at some point. He was staring down at me, wearing his usual smile.

"I can't get my magic to work."

"How about I teach you, then?"

Brother stretched his hand out to me.

I grabbed his outstretched palm…or tried to, before my vision slowly dissipated, and the ceiling came back into view.

Somewhere in the course of my recollection, I'd let my arm drop. I stretched out my hand again, but it met only air. I could no longer see my brother.

This happened on occasion, so I wasn't too surprised. I did, however, have questions. When had Sis sneaked in here?

Freeing myself from her grasp and sacrificing Marianne in my stead, I slowly sat up. Despite my desire to stay there, I managed to wrest myself from the sacred space, the root of my depravity and sloth—my bed—and headed to the window as quietly as I could.

I opened the curtains and window, taking in the fresh breeze while I stretched out my arms and gazed outside. The sun had just peeked up over the horizon, and an empyreal orange glow tinged the half light of the deep-blue sky. There wasn't a cloud in sight.

It was almost a perfect day for running. Apparently, Claris and Nanami had some chores to handle, so they wouldn't be joining me for my early-morning run. There'd be fewer people than usual.

I stretched out one more time and closed the window. I gave a quiet morning greeting to the thing under the bed covers, which was rhythmically heaving up and down, and left the room. Then I headed to the bathroom and washed my face. Just as I started brushing my teeth, a pajama-clad girl walked through the door, rubbing her eyes.

"Oh, morning," I said.

"Ah, Takioto, good morniiiing."

Yawning as she spoke, Yuika came up next to me, then grabbed her light-pink toothbrush and started brushing her teeth.

"Hwooz mwakwig bwokphust whoway?"

"I have absolutely no idea what you're trying to say. Take the brush out, then talk."

"Who's making breakfast today?"

"Claris and Nanami."

I bet I'd get to feast my eyes on Claris wearing an apron instead of her armor if I headed to the kitchen right now. She hadn't always been much of a cook, but her skills had improved by leaps and bounds out of nowhere recently. Her explosion in culinary ability had occurred the same day I cleared the fortieth layer of the Tsukuyomi Academy Dungeon, so maybe it had something to do with the item I'd given her.

That would suggest the seed of possibility improved every aspect of your personhood, not just your combat skills. It would be unwise to jump to conclusions with so few examples, but how great would it be if it was true?

But I digress.

"First thing you're talking about in the morning's breakfast, huh…"

"And what's wrong with that? The Hamburg steak last night was soooooo good. I bet you're just as curious as I am, too!"

"Well, Yukine and I made the Wakoku-style Hamburg steak yesterday, so it was always going to be delicious."

"…Huuuuuh?!"

"What? You're looking at me like I said something ridiculous…"

Hey, sometimes Yukine and I cook, too, you know. Though, it's generally either Marino, Nanami, or Claris.

Yuika had gotten home late, so she must not have seen me working in the kitchen. Maybe she'd been talking with Gabby about something.

"That's 'cause it is ridiculous! Yukine, I can understand, but you, Kousuke Takioto, cooking?!"

She took a step back and looked at me with complete surprise.

"I totally thought Yukine had made that all by herself."

"I taught myself how to cook. There was a time when I wanted to open my own café."

Mumbling a knowing "ahhh," she looked me over from head to toe.

"I guess I miiiight be able to see it. Maybe."

"Right? You should lend a hand if I ever open it up."

"Hmm, I dunnooooo ♪! But if you insist, I'll consider it at ten thousand yen an hour."

Yuika giggled slyly before rubbing her thumb over the tips of her index and middle fingers, as though she was stroking a few bills.

If she worked eight hours a day, her monthly salary would come out to one million and six hundred thousand yen. She'd easily clear ten million before the year was up.

"Are you trying to bleed me dry here? Heck, if I can earn enough to justify handing out a salary like that, then maybe I *should* consider opening up that café."

Yuika may have been going on about getting paid the big bucks, but I got the feeling she'd help me out for a bit without any compensation. That's just the type of person she was.

"Well, we brushed our teeth, so I guess it's time for our run. Yukine's probably waiting for us already," I said.

"Can you hang on a sec? I'm going to change."

"Hmm, I dunnooooo ♪!"

"Bleh, creepy..."

C'mon, I was just copying you. Though, I have to admit it was a little off-putting.

When I left the bathroom to head to the dining table, I saw Ludie sitting on the sofa. She was reading a book on magic, leafing through the pages with a diligent expression on her face.

"Good morning, Ludie."

She lifted her head in response to my voice. Her earrings swayed slightly as she brushed the hair from her eyes.

"Kousuke? Good morning."

"Someone's an eager beaver first thing in the morning. What're you reading?"

"Well, I thought I'd try learning even more advanced-level wind magic, so I went to ask Hatsumi about it, but..."

She trailed off, but I knew what she would say next.

"...I think she's off in dreamland with Marianne right now."

Ludie gave a strained grin, before letting out a small sigh.

"I'll go wake her up in a little bit," she added.

"Good call."

There was no doubt I was benefitting the most from living in the Hanamura house, but Ludie probably had the second most to gain. Marino and Sis were teaching her skills that you would normally have to slog through annoying dungeons to acquire.

"...What're you staring at me like that for?" Ludie asked.

"Oh, sorry. I was just thinking about grabbing some ramen. Going solo's a bit awkward and all."

Ludie bloomed into a rich, honeyed smile, before she replied happily.

"Well, I guess if you really insist. I'll find a time and we can head out together."

I parted ways with Ludie, then poked into the kitchen for a glass of water to find Claris and Nanami standing next to each other, deep in conversation.

"Morning, Nanami. Morning, Claris… Is something wrong?"

"Good morning, Master."

"Good morning, Takioto. We're actually a bit unsure about what to make for breakfast."

"Ah." I nodded.

"What would you prefer, Master? Wakoku, Western, Chinese, Nanami—please pick whatever cuisine you'd like."

"Something's clearly off with one of those options… Hmm, I guess I'll have Wakoku style."

"Got it, Nanami it is. Time to do the nasty work, then."

"So there really wasn't any point in asking me, was there? And why did your voice drop when you said 'nasty'?"

Claris giggled as she watched me and Nanami's usual back-and-forth.

"Please jump in and help me here, Claris."

She must not have been expecting me to rope her into the conversation. "Me?" she asked in surprise, before an idea seemed to pop into her head and a smile suddenly spread across her face.

"*A-ahem.* W-well then, which would you prefer for breakfast—Wakoku, Western, Chinese, or Claris?"

Ah, so she was getting in on it, too, then.

"Hmm, in that case, I'll go with Claris."

"*H-huuuuh?!*"

Claris blushed in confusion. She must have assumed I'd say "Wakoku" again. I managed to guess that she wanted to use Nanami as a reference for the rest of the conversation, too. Unfortunately, that didn't happen.

Nanami whispered something in Claris's ear as she stood quivering. "I see," Claris replied. "W-well, time to do the nasty."

"Um, Claris, if you leave out *work* at the end, it sounds even worse! Let's all just calm down for now. Ludie's in the next room over, and you're going to give her the wrong idea. Obviously, I was just joking!"

"Ah yes, Master, that reminds me—a certain individual said that they have something to discuss with you."

"Who?"

"Someone you know very well. A relative of the man who runs the general store near the station, and a friend of the elderly grocer who the saleslady at the electronics store visits once a week…Ms. Ruija."

I certainly knew her very well! But was the whole lead-up really necessary?

"Well, *that* wasn't easy to parse!"

"How about I put it like this: a relative of the ignoble worm running the general store, and friend to the ignoble worm at the grocer who the ignoble worm at the electronics store visits once a week…an ignoble worm."

"Now you've made everyone an ignoble worm, even Ms. Ruija! I'm so sorry, you all!"

That default setting of hers hadn't changed a bit!

"Only joking, of course. But unfortunately, Ms. Ruija actually does have some business with you."

"…That so, huh. I'm not looking forward to hearing what she wants… Oh well, I'll swing by later."

The pair then returned to discussing breakfast, at which point I departed, making for the garden meetup spot. Yukine was already there.

Clad in her training wear, she was practicing her regular forms with her naginata. A sideways sweep, an upward slash, a downward cut—her ponytail swayed with each movement, and the porcelain nape of her neck was so breathtaking, it deserved to be designated as a national treasure.

"Good morning," I said to her.

"Oh, morning, Takioto. Nice weather today."

If Yuika's smile was provocative and full of energy, like sweetened soda water, then Yukine's was like refreshing citrus.

And so was her personality.

"It got cloudy at the end of the day yesterday. But today's absolutely perfect running weather."

"That's true. The breeze is a bit chilly, but it'll probably feel just right midrun," Yukine said, before closing her eyes and taking a few deep, gentle breaths.

Seeing this, I took some of my own, too. The wind was cold, yes, but I didn't feel it in the sunshine.

"By the way, the Morals Committee members seemed to be interested in you, Takioto. Can you pop in if you've got a chance?"

"Oh, sure, of course. There's someone there I want to see anyway," I responded, prompting her to cock her head.

"Someone you want to see…? Who's that? Captain Stef?"

"Who else would I want to see but you, Yukine?"

"Oh, you meant me… Wait, m-me…?! You f-fool!"

I felt a bit embarrassed at having made the comment as I watched Yukine avert her eyes, clearly pleased despite her protests.

"I'm kidding. I want to see both you and Ludie. Now, how far are we going today?"

"…You're heading into a dungeon today, right? Let's go with a lighter, twenty-five-mile route today."

"*Huuuuh?!*"

That interjection prompted Yukine and me to turn around.

There stood Yuika. She'd changed into shorts and leggings to make the run more comfortable.

"Ludie warned me that your notion of 'lighter' is seriously way outta whack."

Yukine and I both glanced at each other. Such beauty.

"Really?" I asked.

"Yes, really, sheesh… I'll still go out with you until the end, though," she said.

"All right, but don't push yourself too hard."

"Who do you think I am? This'll be nothing, no sweat at all… Oh, right. Takioto."

"What now?"

"Saying 'go out with you' actually reminded me."

"Whoa, hold up. You can't talk about us like that in front of Yukine; that's sensitive stuff."

"Apologies. Just a joke."

Yukine had to have known that was a joke, right? She was shooting me a seriously disgusted glare, though.

"I want to go to the Ceremonial Committee today, so I'm wondering if you'd take me along."

"To the Ceremonial Committee?"

"Yup, that's the place. I wanted to thank Minister Benito in person, and when I messaged him about it, he said he had something he wanted to talk with me about, too."

"So Minister Benito has business with you, huh…"

"Hmm…"

At this, Yukine folded her arms and seemed to lapse into thought. What was it about, though? Maybe she was concerned about the whole Gabby situation.

"Got it. What time?" I asked.

"I should be asking you instead. When are you free?"

"How about we do it after morning classes, then? Don't be shy about my reward now," I jokingly added.

"Seriously? Ugh, I guess I have to. I'll give you some tickets for a free shoulder rub."

"Aw, sweet! Working at a computer all day's got my eyes strained, and my shoulders are stiffer than mithril. No joke, the slightest movement makes them crack and pop like no tomorrow—not! Like hell I need that! What are you, an elementary school kid on Father's Day?!"

"Hmm, your retort sure had a lot of realness to it."

Yukine didn't know this, of course, but I'd gotten the full office-worker experience in my last life! But hang on. There's something sorta sexy about the combination of "beautiful girl" and "free shoulder-rub tickets," right?! More like shoulder RUB (really, unquestionably bawdy).

"Okay then, I'll draw your portrait with the words *thank you* written on the bottom."

"Ahh, fine, that'll do. Heck, that's something I'd want anyway, so now I'm curious."

"Wait, you're seriously okay with that? All right, then, I'll whip up the portrait during class for you."

"Whoa there. You gotta pay attention in class."

When I pointed this out to Yuika, she stared at me as if she couldn't believe her ears.

"Excuuuuse me?! You're the last person who should be saying that. Seeing you in class is like encountering a rare spawn."

"'Rare spawn'?! What d'ya mean, 'rare spawn'?!" I asked.

Yukine started to chuckle as Yuika and I continued our back-and-forth.

"Hee-hee-hee…"

"What is it, Yukine?"

"Ah, sorry. It just occurred to me that this must be what happiness is like."

I casually glanced at Yuika. She was probably wondering where the heck the sentiment had come from all of a sudden. But I deeply empathized with what Yukine was feeling.

"All right, then, Takioto, Yuika. Time to get running!"

"Got it," I said, looking up at the sky. Ahh, what beautiful weather. There wasn't a cloud overhead.

Generally speaking, the student body didn't have warm feelings for their peers in the Ceremonial Committee. Not that I held this against them, since we did act like their enemies and all.

However, this wasn't true for the people who were aware of what was really going on, like the other Three Committees members and the teachers. That also went for my classmate Orange, who knew me really well—he continued to interact with me like nothing had changed.

Nevertheless, one of my classmates, a girl named Katorina who wore her pink hair in pigtails, grimaced as she looked at me.

"Why the hell are you here?"

Is it just me, or was that a super-rude way to greet someone?

"This is the first time we've seen each other in ages, and that's all you've got to say to me?" I asked.

"You did cross paths the other day, technically," Nanami chimed in. Sure, I could see Katorina all the time if I went to class like I was supposed to, but I was usually holed up in a dungeon.

"What do you expect when you basically never show up? Orange has even started saying stuff like 'I caught a glimpse of Takioto; today's gonna be my lucky day,'" Katorina said.

What was I, the bluebird of happiness or something? I guess what Yuika had said was true—I may as well have been a rare spawn in the eyes of the regular students. Though, the fact that I was with the Ceremonial Committee meant they'd probably think I was *bad* luck, if anything.

"Forget about what Orange thinks. Don't you skip school, like, *too* much?" Katorina asked.

"I do *technically* come to school, though."

Katorina and I just never saw each other because our schedules never lined up or I was at the Moon Palace.

"Sure. By the way, you joined *the* Ceremonial Committee, right?"

"Yup, sure did," I said, puffing out my chest. After mumbling an "ahhh," Katorina continued…

"That something I can congratulate you on, or?"

…cocking her head as she spoke.

"Of course you can. It's nothing but smooth sailing from here on out."

"Kudos to you, then," she said sarcastically, averting her eyes and giving a huff. I knew what this was supposed to be. It was her clumsy way of giving me her blessing.

"Appreciate it. How've you been lately?"

"Things have been going great thanks to a certain somebody. Though, sometimes, it annoys me to think I'm just your charity case," she said, staring me in the face. She must've been working through the dungeon I'd told her about.

"I wasn't trying to be charitable or anything."

"Hearing that's also annoying. Like, the way you say it or something. I wonder why?"

"Aren't you being a little *too* harsh here?"

"Anyways, I heard some stuff at the Student Council."

The Student Council, huh.

"So, like, you're spreading all sorts of info about dungeons around, right?"

Well, she got me there.

"They said that there's a lot of people who've benefited from this favor of yours. Even the vice president said it was useful to her. And so, well, that sorta got me thinking."

She eyed me with a scowl.

"Why're you telling everyone about all this?"

"Because I want everyone to get nice and strong—why else? Then once they're nice and powerful, I'll stand up on top of 'em all. Awesome, right?"

"Suuure… I really don't get what's going through your head."

"That's seriously the entire reason, so wondering about it isn't gonna get you anywhere. That aside, you mentioned that you heard that from the Student Council, yeah?"

Maybe they had already approached her? I went to ask as much, but Katorina interrupted me before I got the chance.

"I just go into the dungeon with them sometimes, that's all. Well, they also force some annoying minor stuff on me, too, occasionally... Hold on, you aren't getting any funny ideas, are you? I'm just doing some odd jobs, okay?"

Would "odd jobs" have her visiting the Moon Palace? It seemed like my hunch was right on the money.

"I was just about to head over there myself. Got some business with the Three Committees," I said.

"Hmmm, that's fine, then. Now's as good a time as ever, so I've got something I want to say to you, too."

"What?"

"I heard that Yuika really had a rough time, right? And you saved her."

Had Katorina heard that from Iori, who she hung out with a lot, or from Yuika herself?

"Yeah, we managed somehow."

"Don't worry Ludie and everyone like that."

Now this was a familiar feeling. Despite how she may have come off, Katorina really looked out for others.

"...Were you also concerned about me?"

"Yeah right, stupid. Like I'd ever worry about you. Besides."

"Besides?"

"Hearing that you went through the Tsukuyomi Dungeon got me thinking. Soloing all that? It's absolutely bonkers. So I knew nothing was going to take you down."

I had to admit that I couldn't really complain if the average person saw me as crazy.

"Plus, if you're going to lose to anyone, it's going to be me," she asserted.

"*Pfft.*"

"Don't you laugh. I'm serious. Pretty soon... Oh well, forget it. You'll find out later."

"Huh, hold up, what are you talking about?"

"Nothing, okay?!"

Katorina turned around and walked off in the direction I had just come from. Then she called out to me, as though suddenly remembering something.

"Ah, right. If you're ever in a bind, like back when Yuika was in trouble, give me a shout. I may not be much help, though."

"C'mon, what're you talking about? You'd be a huge help. I'll come calling if something comes up. And don't you worry—I'll come running if you're ever in trouble, too."

Just as she'd waved her hand and made to leave again, Katorina came to a halt, then muttered, "...Idiot," before heading off.

"She's come down with a severe case of *tsundere*. I can see it clear as day. Katorina felt her chest ready to burst with love for you, Master, so she couldn't help but flee. Of that, there is no doubt."

"Just don't say that in front of her, okay?"

Nanami may have gone a bit too far, but I couldn't deny the tsundere part. For some reason, Katorina was sensitive about it.

From there, we walked along together until Nanami clapped her hands, as if she had just remembered something.

"Master, there's something I'd like to ask you."

"What?"

"I've ascertained that there are even more improvements that can be added to the treadmill you've been working out on and would like to discuss possible enhancements."

"Yuika would get seriously pissed if she heard about this."

On the other hand, Yukine seemed to be really into it, and she used it all the time. To my delight, she'd even set me as her Main Butler. She'd gotten this bashful little look when she did it, too.

"I actually added new experimental functionality. Want to guess what it is?"

"I feel like it's already got enough bells and whistles as is. What, is it going to, like, hand you a drink or something?"

Or maybe it would automatically deliver you towels or something. That would be really convenient if she could pull it off.

"Brilliant as always, Master—BAAM. You have a truly sharp eye for these things. I am honored to serve as your stunningly beautiful personal maid. Indeed, I wish Ruija would learn a thing or two from your esteemed example. Look at him go, a master of the world."

"Y-you think so?"

"Of course. And it's just as you said: The new functionality I am planning on adding is a battle mode."

"You laid the praise on real thick, but I wasn't remotely on the mark. *Drink* and *battle* don't even share any letters!"

Better yet, what was up with this "master of the world" business?

"Rest assured, the base has already been completed, and Miss Yukine is test-running four of the courses. You'll be able to square off against nonplayer characters equipped with the latest cutting-edge AI."

"You're telling me someone other than Sis got dragged into this?!"

What in the world was Yukine doing?!

"To spice things up, I've also built a mechanic into the mode where eating poisonous-looking mushrooms will increase your speed."

That's just *M*rio Kart*!

"I'm smelling some bad news here. Is this okay? Are we going to get sued?"

Now that Nanami mentioned it, this world actually had its own version of *M*rio Kart*, too. I mean, there is a heroine in *MX* who plays a *Monster H*nter* clone, so I guess it wasn't weird to have a *M*rio Kart* clone, too. In fact, this sort of popular video game parody was a real staple of the eroge genre.

"It will be fine. We're going with the explanation that ingesting the mushroom induces an aroused and delirious state in the central nervous system, increasing your acceleration."

"That's even more alarming! Those are straight up magic freaking mushrooms, aren't they?! Make it so the mushrooms improve the engine combustion or something instead!"

The original game also has a mushroom that turns you giant, which is a whole lot more *yikes* if you think about it, huh?

"I also created a mode where there was a chance that children would jump into the road chasing a ball, or bikes would suddenly swerve into your path, but it was rejected since it resulted in nonstop collisions."

"The hell is that, a driver's ed simulation or something?"

It felt like the developers of those things crammed every possible roadside danger in Japan into a single block. The background characters clearly had a death wish, too, which just amplified the chaos.

"I also happened to acquire multiple machines utilizing the same system, so it's now possible to battle opponents remotely."

"What the heck? That actually sounds sorta fun."

"This is where the favor I would like to ask you comes in, Master."

"What is it?"

"As I am finding myself shorthanded, I'm thinking about forming a group to assist me in an unofficial capacity. I would like to employ several people, if possible."

"Just what in the world are you up to…? Don't do anything that'll inconvenience people, got it?"

At times like these, my obliviousness about how active Nanami was never failed to cross my mind. Actually, hold it—didn't we spend almost all our time together?

"Of course. I'm aiming for our Nanami Factory to have the highest production numbers in the world."

"I'm a little nervous about this, but it'll work out, right?"

"For now, I've given my word, so I'll be building my support team. Don't go complaining about it later."

"I've got a terrible feeling about this…"

We continued to banter nonsensically as we headed toward the spot where we were meeting Yuika.

We linked up with Yuika not long after parting ways with Katorina.

"Thanks again for this," she said.

"Yup, just leave it to me."

Yuika had business with the Ceremonial Committee, and I was acting as her guide. That being said, I was planning on having her find the rest of the way herself once we passed through entrance security.

"How was class today?" I asked Yuika.

"Well, let me tell you, I drew a truly wonderful picture: a tiny version of you with his arms up in the air, smiling against the backdrop of a bright and sunny day."

"So my comment about you being an elementary schooler was on the mark after all!"

"I'm kidding, obviously. Really. My drawing came out so spectacular that I can't help bragging about it. No one else could hold a candle to me."

Hearing this, Nanami grinned.

"Is that so…? It appears the time has come for Master Painter Nanami to flaunt her skills, then."

"This is definitely the first I've heard of this," I said.

Not once in my life had I heard anyone describe Nanami as a master painter. That being said, she did seem like she would have a knack for it. But I bet Katorina was just as awful at drawing as I was.

Still babbling back and forth, we headed out, when Yuika suddenly fell silent.

I followed her gaze and instantly understood why. Glancing back at her, I saw that she had an ab-so-lutely loathsome expression on her face.

The object of her glare, Gabriella, also looked like she'd just encountered her mortal enemy.

"Fate, perhaps," Nanami muttered. If fate had brought us here, then it must have been cruel indeed. At least to these two.

However, the two girls were quite far away from each other at the moment. Either one was in a position to take an alternate path to avoid the other, but the question was whether they'd actually do it.

Nah, there was no way they were backing down. Not Gabriella, whose pride—and only her pride—was on par with Monica of the Big Three, nor Yuika, who could have a serious stubborn streak. Yup, wasn't happening.

"Ah, good day to you, Kousuke Takioto, Yuika Hijiri, and, um…the maid. For a second there, I thought saw a terrible blight on the scenery, but it seems it was just you three," Gabriella remarked.

She couldn't come up with Nanami's name. Given how incredibly popular Nanami was on campus, I would have figured she had heard about her before.

"Ohhhh, good morning! I thought some trash had come into view for a moment there, but it was just you, Gabriella! Sorry for mistaking you for garbage. But on second thought, what's the difference?"

What the hell were these two doing? It had taken all of an instant for them to start holding a mudslinging competition.

"*Gaaaaaaah*, you are so reprehensibly ill-mannered!"

Uh, Gabby, you were pretty offensive yourself there. I definitely couldn't point that out to her right now, though.

"Excuuuse me? Like you have a leg to stand on, either!"

"Both of you, just calm down…"

Gabby shot a glare at me after I spoke up to stop them. She inhaled deeply, then took a step back.

"I've been doing some thinking."

"About what?" I asked.

"A simple competition between us would be far too droll, wouldn't you agree? Let's throw in a penalty to spice things up."

"What do you mean, 'penalty'?"

"Listen well, Kousuke Takioto. If you lose, I want you to step down as assistant vice-minister and prostrate yourself before me. For you, Yuika, the prostration alone will suffice."

"Huuuh?! There's no way Takioto would agree to those conditions!"

"But in return, should I lose to either of you...I'll leave this school."

Hold up a second. Drop out of the Academy?! Why?!

"Neither of us stands to gain anything from you leaving, though," I pointed out.

"You think I'm an eyesore, do you not? Under these stipulations, you won't have to interact with me again should the worst transpire. That's quite a benefit, I would say. What is it, then? Are you frightened of losing?"

"Wha—? I'm not scared at all! That's not the problem."

"Well then, I do not see what the issue could be."

"But still, what's up with you wagering your place at school...? What's going on, Gabriella?'

"I am obliged to become ceremonial minister, no matter the cost. Hence why I need to give a proper showing of my talents and abilities."

Had something happened between Gabby and Minister Benito? It felt like she was going off the deep end.

"But the terms matter not—it's inconceivable I could lose. You needn't worry about a thing."

"And Minister Benito's given you the go-ahead?"

"I have, in fact, already received his permission. All that remains is your consent to the terms."

I couldn't believe it—what the heck was Minister Benito thinking to agree to this?

Argh, this was a real predicament. Given Gabby's personality, the wrong choice here could send things in a bad direction. If her future was being laid in my hands, then what I needed to do here was...

"Fine, I can see you're serious about this, Gabriella. I accept your challenge."

"Takioto?!"

Confusion was all over Yuika's face.

"Do you think I'm going to lose?" I asked her.

"Of course I don't! But that's not the point!"

"Then what's the problem?" I said, before turning back to Gabby. "Let's do this. But if we're going to compete, I want to add a condition of my own."

"And what would that be?"

"If I win, you have to do whatever I say. Just once."

A look of befuddlement came over Gabriella, but then she quickly wrapped her arms around her chest. She followed up by flashing a sharp glare my way.

"...Yes, yes, that's quite all right. Make me dance naked, turn me into your slave, whatever you wish. I won't be losing to you either way."

"Whoa, whoa, wait a second. Takioto! What sort of deviant nonsense is going through your head?! Don't make me report you!"

Why did the two of you both assume I had something perverted in mind here? Okay, okay, I couldn't deny that I was a pervert. But that's beside the point.

"All right, then let's throw down," I said.

"Indeed, you'd best prepare yourself. Feel free to run away with your tail between your legs; it doesn't bother me in the slightest. I'll simply take over as assistant vice-minister instead," Gabriella said before walking off. I could only sigh as she let out bursts of haughty laughter—perhaps from imagining her own victory—as she departed.

...So it had come to this. The circumstances were a bit weird, but what exactly had Minister Benito gotten up to?

While I pondered this, Yuika continued to grumble quietly to herself. After calming down a little bit, she heaved a sigh like a tired old man.

"Sheesh, what's going to happen if Gabby loses...?"

"Don't worry, leave it to me."

I had no intention of making Gabby drop out.

"...Ahhh, right. My sign had the best fortune today, right?" Yuika said.

"Yes, you did indeed. Your lucky color was red, yes," Nanami replied. I had forgotten she was even there. For once, she hadn't butted into the conversation with her teasing and jokes.

Incidentally, my luck wasn't all that great, but I had won the morning-horoscope show's rock-paper-scissors match.

"Fortunes are never reliable, are they?"

"That's 'cause there's no telling how they'll play out."

I didn't put any stock in that stuff, but for some reason, I was still happy to have come out on top. Though, there were some people who didn't believe their daily fortunes at all except for the days when they were said to be the luckiest.

"Do you care about horoscopes and such?" I asked Yuika.

"Well, I don't really pay too much attention to them, but…I feel like the fortunes Ms. Sakura tells have a bit of credibility."

"Oh, Ms. Sakura the librarian?"

"Yeah, her. Ms. Sakura's fortunes really do come true, you know. She managed to predict what would happen to Iori down to a surprising amount of detail."

"Really?"

"Yup, and not just once, but twice."

"Huh. Do you have Ms. Sakura read your fortune a lot?"

"No, just every now and then. Iori's been secretly rendezvousing with her quite a lot from what I can tell, so he might be having her read his fortune more often."

"*Secret rendezvous*… What a splendid turn of phrase. I'd love to have one with Master," Nanami interjected.

If you're talking about the two of us seeing each other, Nanami, that happens like every day.

"Uuuggh… I have so much to do after this, and now I'm feeling all out of whack…," Yuika groaned.

"Hey, c'mon, you're about to head over and see the elder Evangelista in the Ceremonial Committee," I said.

Yuika had mentioned something or other about wanting to thank him for helping her out when she was abducted, right? Minister Benito said he had some business with her, too, so it was perfect timing, really.

But seriously, what did Minister Benito want with her? It had to be about Gabriella if Yuika was involved. Or maybe he was inviting her to the Ceremonial Committee?

"Yeah, I'll be sure to cool down by then. Sorry, Takioto."

"Don't worry about it."

Technically, this had all happened because she stood up for me. I'd have to treat her to something later.

"Oh, yes, Master?" Nanami said.

"Hmm, what is it?"

"I shall gladly do whatever you say whenever you want. If you order me to lift up my skirt, then I'll—"

"Okay, let's get outta here."

The Moon Palace housed the headquarters for the Student Council, Morals Committee, and Ceremonial Committee, so regular students weren't typically allowed inside. It was often used to discuss things that the general student population wasn't supposed to hear or to hold meetings.

For those reasons, you end up going there pretty often in the game, whether it's to invite someone in the Three Committees to join your dungeon party, or to view some event or another. Basically, if you're looking for someone in the Three Committees, chances are they'll be at the Moon Palace.

Once I escorted Yuika to the Ceremonial Committee, I headed for the Morals Committee room.

Inside was a single male student. Nanami bowed to him.

"Yo, how's it going?" he said.

This guy was one of the male characters in the Morals Committee. All the Three Committees had male members, but they were few and far between. Harsh but fair, considering this was an eroge world.

"Hello, Holger."

Naturally, every last one of them had their own romantic partners or were uninterested in dating to ensure nothing would happen between them and the heroines.

I mean, think about it. If a game came out where you could get cucked by another character without advance warning, there was no doubt the intense player backlash would be talked about for years to come.

Also, I honestly wished developers would refrain from making the heroines betray you and never come back, for both my mental health and my party's strength (tears of blood, seriously).

"Anyways, I don't have much on my plate right now," I told him.

"*Gah-hah-hah!* Glad to hear it."

Holger was tall, muscular, and had a shaved head. Eroge players had dubbed him "Baldy" without a second thought.

"If something ever comes up, you better let me know now, ya hear?"

"Thank you. I was actually looking to ask about something. How's Ludie been?"

"Tréfle, huh? She's a wonderful girl. Her abilities are two heads above the rest of the first-years, and she'd stand toe to toe with some of the second-years, too."

"Above all else, her extreme diligence is a sight to behold," someone else chimed in.

My heart skipped a beat at the voice.

I immediately turned to the person who'd interjected and saw a beautiful woman carrying a large shield on her back.

"Nice to meet you, Esmeralda. I'm Kousuke Takioto. And this is..."

"His maid, Nanami."

Ohhhhhh yeah, it was Ironwall. Ironwall! *The* Ironwall herself.

A beauty whose upturned eyes and slightly fierce expression belie how she enjoys comedy, *loves* animals, and tearfully tells a puppy she finds abandoned in a cardboard box that she can't take it in because she lives in a dorm, only to find it a foster home—*that* Ironwall.

"You already know me, do you? I'm Esmeralda. It's a pleasure to meet you, Takioto and Nanami. I've been hearing about you for some time now...and was eagerly awaiting the day when our paths would cross."

She held her hand out toward me. After I returned her shake, she turned and held her hand out to Nanami, who immediately exchanged handshakes with her as well.

"I'm pleased just hearing that the Shield of the Morals Committee remembers my name. I still have a lot to learn, but I look forward to working together," I said.

As her appearance suggested, Esmeralda, the Ironwall of the Morals Committee, was a tank, a character who excelled at taking attacks. Defensively, she was on par with the Big Three, and she was the main reason why players would swap out Takioto and Baldy (aka Holger) from their parties.

"And I as well."

"So has Ludie already gotten started on Morals Committee work?"

"Yup. A fight broke out between some students where magic was involved…but she brilliantly resolved the situation."

The Morals Committee's goal was to preserve peace and safety on campus. In the event that a magical conflict broke out, it swiftly intervened to put a stop to things.

"Miss Ludie never fails to impress," Nanami chimed in.

In-game, these sorts of disputes trigger a fight with the students. Except for some reason, the students always end up forming a tag team against you, despite the fact that they were arguing against each other in the first place. Why two people who were about to come to blows would join together as one to fight *you*, the world may never know.

"Speak of the devil…"

Ludie, Yukine, and the Saint entered the room.

"Captain Stef…welcome back. You too, Yukine and Ludie."

The Saint glanced at me briefly and gave a dispassionate greeting.

"Good day to you, Kousuke Takioto. I'm sorry, but there's something I have to finish up right away."

Then she headed into the room in the back.

Meanwhile, Ludie and Yukine came up to us.

"What, pray tell, can we do for you, Kousuke? As it happens, we were just having a conversation about you before we arrived."

Ludie was still putting on her refined-princess routine. I was sure it wouldn't be long before it disappeared.

"Oh, I had something I wanted to run by the Saint. I wonder if she'll be long… Maybe I should come back another time."

Yukine shook her head.

"Nah, Captain Stef will be finished soon. Go ahead and talk to her after. But anyways…"

"Hmm?"

"…there's something I'd like to ask you to do in a bit."

"Today works fine. I made a promise to see Ivy, so it'll have to be after that."

"It's not urgent, so it can wait. The thing is, I want you to bring Ludie to Magistrate Anemone. The two of them will probably have many occasions to work together from here on out, so I figured introductions wouldn't hurt. You know her really well, right?"

That caught me off guard. I would have never expected to hear Sexy

Scientist's name coming out of Yukine's mouth. But it was true—I probably knew that woman better than anyone else.

"Hmmm, well, I guess if had to say one way or the other, I do know her. And there is something I want to ask her, too, so…I don't necessarily mind introducing Ludie to her, but…"

"But?" Ludie replied, cocking her head.

"The truth is, I haven't actually met her yet. In fact, I haven't seen anyone else show up to the Ceremonial Committee besides Shion and Minister Benito before."

"I see it's business as usual at the Ceremonial Committee, then."

"Yup, that's the Ceremonial Committee for you."

Both Esmeralda and Holger smiled ironically.

"…I wonder if it'll be okay… Actually, *you* should be fine," Yukine said to me.

"I'll be all right. I've heard the rumors."

Sexy Scientist had an unbelievably eccentric personality. Who knows what would happen if Ludie went to see her by herself?

"So do you really not mind?"

"Nope, not at all."

"You haven't met her before, right, Ludie?"

"Not quite," Ludie muttered in reply to my question. "I have met her before, but…only long enough for a cursory exchange of pleasantries."

Both women hailed from the same country, and Anemone was technically nobility herself, which explained how their paths had crossed.

"She's incredibly intelligent and capable, but whether she's respectable or not is a different story…," Yukine grumbled. That may have been the average person's evaluation of Anemone, but we eroge players definitely respected her.

"I'd say Benito's done a great job organizing everyone together."

"He's quite superb, not to mention an excellent role model," Esmeralda said, nodding.

"If only you had been able to join the Ceremonial Committee," Holger murmured, rubbing his, let's say, *defenseless* head.

"You wanted to join the Ceremonial Committee, Esmeralda?"

She nodded at Ludie's question.

"Yes, I would have liked to work under Minister Benito's leadership…"

"She's his one true believer."

"I wouldn't go so far as to call myself a 'true believer,' but I do think he's a very fine person… If there's anyone I look up to, it's the ceremonial minister."

"That's a surprise. Here I was sure you looked up to President Monica."

"President Monica obviously has many wonderful qualities, from her leadership ability to her intelligence to her individual strength, but the ceremonial minister is admirable in a different way."

"What do you mean?"

"As part of the Ceremonial Committee, he shows more consideration to the student body than any other. He is compassionate and looks out for people. And though his strength may not equal Monica's, he is still very powerful himself. He would be well qualified to be the president of either the Morals Committee or the Student Council. And *yet*!" she said, emphasizing "yet."

"Minister Benito instead elected to join the Ceremonial Committee. He has endured all manner of conflict as a member of the students' symbolic enemy. I've seen him endure scathing derision myself."

She continued even further.

"I am sure that he's experienced many trying moments I'm not aware of, too. Yet he has played his role with what can only be described as perfection! All while nonchalantly pretending like it was nothing!"

"*Gwa-ha-ha*, we get that you respect him a lot, so take it down a notch," Holger said.

"M-my apologies. All that is to say, that's why I'm a bit jealous of you, Takioto."

Esmeralda intensely respected Minister Benito, but she still insisted that she had not an ounce of romantic feelings for him. It seemed like that was true, too. As far as I could tell, he didn't have any feelings for her, either.

"You never considered joining the Ceremonial Committee yourself, Miss Esmeralda?" Nanami asked.

"I understood that being on the Ceremonial Committee would be particularly difficult for someone of my character…"

Indeed, Esmeralda had a strong sense of justice, and she wasn't good at lying, either. Her personality wasn't a good fit for the Ceremonial Committee. But that was also part of what made Esmeralda so lovely.

"Sorry, but could we get back to the topic at hand?" Yukine asked, prompting an apology from Esmeralda.

"Now, back to Magistrate Anemone. She's, well, very unique. I was worried about having Ludie go alone, but I'm sure it'll be fine with you and Nanami accompanying her. Thanks," Yukine told me.

Honestly, part of me felt like Nanami and Anemone would create some bizarre chemical reaction and bring about a brave new world, but...things would probably work out.

"No problem. Anyway, do you think Captain Stef's finished up with whatever she had to do?"

"She was just receiving a report over the phone, so she should be free now. I'll go along with you."

Casually saying good-bye to the others, Yukine, Nanami, and I went to where we could find the Saint—her personal chambers, the office of the president of the Morals Committee.

She'd finished the task she needed to handle and was browsing through her Tsukuyomi Traveler while sipping coffee.

However, it seemed my arrival wasn't exactly cause for celebration, for she blatantly sighed when I headed into the room.

"Oh, it's you. Hello. I can't offer you anything, but come on in."

She gave us a truly indifferent and curt reception, a far cry from the Saint's usual feigned friendliness. The regular students would probably faint if they saw her like this.

I looked at Yukine, who pulled out a chair, urging me to take a seat. Nanami seemed intent on remaining standing, but there was a possibility our conversation could go on for a while, so I had her sit down as well.

"Thank you very much," I told Stef.

"Well, I suppose I should at least start by congratulating you on being named assistant vice-minister. Be sure to work hard now, future Ceremonial Minister."

"Thank you very much. I'm aware that I am unworthy of such an important position, but I'll give my all to live up to the honor."

"...Sure."

"Oh, Takioto. The captain isn't actually angry. You can let your guard down," Yukine told me.

"That's right, I'm not upset or anything. Though, I am a bit shocked to hear you can be so polite."

I could be certain she was, in fact, not angry. She was simply indifferent toward me. Though considering her circumstances, I could understand what would make her so indifferent.

"Now, what brings you to my office today?"

"I simply wanted to stop by and formally introduce myself, as well as talk about some future courses of action."

"Hmm. So I assume this is about how you're going to conduct yourself?"

"I'm glad we can get straight to the point."

"I may as well hear it, then. However, there is one thing I'd like to say first."

"And what might that be?"

"I don't really care what you do. But can you avoid giving us any extra trouble? You Ceremonial Committee people certainly love doing as you please, but I wish you'd be more considerate of our end of things. It's annoying."

She was exactly right.

"Yes, I apologize for my previous behavior that forced you to restrict access to the school dungeon. Rest assured that I will consult with you whenever I make any major moves in the future."

"You seem to get it, at least, so that'll do…," the Saint said, giving me a hard stare up and down.

Saint Stef was a beautiful woman. Attractive enough to have her own fan club. Though to be fair, almost *every* character who featured in an eroge was going to be cute and pretty.

It was slightly embarrassing to have someone so beautiful give me a once-over, yet it was also a little arousing. But why exactly was she scrutinizing me so intently?

"So you don't think anything about me right now?" the Saint asked.

"What I think? Well, I think you're a wonderful woman. Normally, you're elegant and ladylike, but right now, I can see a strength within that beauty, and it makes you even more attractive."

"Listen, you…"

Perhaps my answer was a little bit too glib.

"Oh, you meant what I think about your *attitude*, did you? Hmm, well, I'm happy to have glimpsed yet another side of you."

My comments had probably veered in a completely unexpected

direction to her. Saint Stef let out a heavy sigh before holding her hand to her temple.

"...You say the same sort of things as Benito."

I could not but laud his tact. I could crack jokes because I knew her so well, but then what about Minister Benito? He had quite the nerve to say stuff like that to her. I mean, if he wasn't careful, he could be fixed with a downright polar glare that would freeze me solid.

Though now that I think about it, Minister Benito was Leggenze nobility himself, so he might be somewhat familiar with her. Anyone who knew her circumstances would want to try doing something to help her.

Given his position in society, Minister Benito should have become an enemy during the Saint's events in the game. Yet instead, he stands by her side. He's actually one of the characters who cooperates the most with her, along with the Student Council president.

When all is said and done, though, he still claims that "he has no romantic feelings" for the Saint. Really? None at all?

"...Talking to you throws me off-kilter, that's for sure. Anyway, what can I help you with?"

After the Saint sighed, she'd continued on and changed the subject.

"Yes, well, I was doing some thinking about how I should spend my time on campus going forward...but the conclusion I arrived at is sort of, well... I thought I'd need to run it by you first."

"Sort of...what, exactly?"

"To be honest, I was considering teasing the other girls in the Three Committees like I just did with you now, along with taking the liberty of hitting on them and stuff."

The air instantly froze. I had answered in a way that could be uncharitably interpreted, so you could say that I'd cooled things down myself.

"Do you mind repeating that?"

"...What's your angle here?"

Yukine was glaring at me like I was a shady criminal. Honestly, I was eating it up.

"To be more specific, I thought I'd make it look like I was trying to chat up and seduce the girls in the Three Committees."

"...I want to hear why."

"Well, looking at myself objectively here, I think people see me as a

guy who keeps making passes at Ludie while he has his cute maid follow along behind him."

At this stage anyway.

"Oh, Master. 'Cute maid'? Come now... I'll have to go with Nanami
Special B today, won't I? Time to get the toothpicks and rope ready."

"And here I thought you were showing interest in my plan. Could
you cool it with the suggestive remarks? There are people who'll actually get the wrong idea here."

Mainly the Saint. She was already totally disgusted. But hey, this was
going just how Nanami and I had drawn it up.

Though, I was unironically curious about what this whole "Nanami
Special B" thing was. What on earth were the toothpicks and rope
for?

"...Um, setting Nanami's dumb joke aside for now, that's seriously
how the other students see me. And that's when it hit me—why don't I
actually use that to my advantage?"

Why not just accept how people saw me at this point? I'd just play
the part of a flirting womanizer. That was the strategy.

"It won't be unnatural to have either Ludie or you, Yukine, with me
from here on out, right? So I can make them all think, *Is this asshole
following them around and hitting on them again?*"

The Saint murmured in acknowledgment, though her expression
looked entirely uninterested.

"Hmm, that might be a better method than I thought... You can give
the impression to outsiders that Yukine and the others can't outright
refuse your advances since you're a member of the Hanamura family,
and that they're just going along with you out of obligation. Make them
think, *I feel so bad for the girls—Kousuke Takioto is so annoying.* But
what're you going to do if that causes problems?"

"That was why I thought I'd hit on students involved with the Three
Committees. With the Student Council or Morals Committee nearby,
none of the other students are going to make any moves. It'll serve as
a slight bit of deterrence, won't it?"

"I get it," Yukine said. "With us around, we can 'warn' Takioto to help
cool everybody down if things start getting out of hand..."

"Right, and this will allow us to incite anger while keeping the area
somewhat under control."

The important thing was that it wouldn't be unnatural to have Yukine or Ludie with me.

The Saint raised her head, as if she'd remembered something.

"Hold on a minute… You're saying you'd be pretending to hit on the female members of the Three Committees, right?"

"Yeah. You have your own fan club, Saint Stef, so you and the Student Council president would be first on the list. Well, first on a list that doesn't include Yukine or Ludie, since I want to move around with them anyway. Leave it to me. My fake pickup-artist routine will bring a smile to your face. Just you watch."

The Saint made no attempt to hide her utter disgust.

"There's one other thing I need to say ahead of time, but… Yukine, Nanami," I started.

"What?"

"Could you leave us alone for a few minutes?"

"…Okay."

"Call for us immediately if you feel like you're in any danger, Saint Stefania."

"Have some faith in Master…"

After watching the two leave the room, the Saint sighed.

"Well then, what is this thing that is so important, you needed the other two to leave?"

"May I ask you a question first, Saint?"

"…And what would that be?" she replied, looking like she truly couldn't be bothered to care.

"What do you think 'freedom' is?"

"Why on earth are you asking me something like that?"

"Sorry, but I really wanted to ask you… You don't have to respond if you don't want to."

"…You're that eager, huh? Fine. I don't exactly know what you're trying to get at here, but freedom refers to all the people like you."

"Then what do you think about the way you are currently?"

I must have struck a bit of a nerve. Her eyebrows twitched.

"And why do I have to tell you that?"

She's right, I thought.

"How about I put it like this—are you enjoying yourself at the moment?"

"......"

The Saint didn't reply, but I knew the answer, of course.

"See, me, I'm having fun. I want everyone around me to be laughing and smiling, too."

"...Imposing your fantasy and ideals on others, are we?"

"Yes, I understand that. Which is why I've been scrambling to build up strength."

Despite knowing the risks, I had gone into the Tsukuyomi Dungeon to make this dream a reality.

"I don't really get what you're talking about, but a pinch of power isn't going to accomplish anything. You may be able to help some people with it, sure. But you can forget about saving everyone. Why? Because there's a tremendous evil out there in the world that can't be stopped."

"Oh, I'm well aware. And the people all truly believe in that evil, too. That's what makes it so nasty, really."

Saint Stef says these exact words in the game, which explained why she was now taken aback. But I continued pelting her with questions.

"What do you think about the current Saint system yourself?"

She looked too shocked to think coherently. Little wonder, when barely anyone should have been familiar with the workings of the system.

"Personally, I think it's a load of bullshit. So allow me to say this—I'm going to crush this evil straight from the source."

"Hold on! What are you talking about...? Or rather, what do you know?"

Had Yukine ever seen the Saint so flustered before? I had my doubts.

"Just about everything, I'd say... That goes for the future, too."

"The future...? Listen, you..."

We already had the key to saving Saint Stef—Yuika, a direct descendent of the Founding Saint. Now the only thing we needed was strength. Once we obtained that power, I was going to save her, no matter what. I had resolved to do just that back under the waterfall.

"In the future, you're smiling. From the depths of your heart."

That version of Stefania was the best of them all. Before she could say something back, I turned right around and left the room.

Nanami and Yukine were waiting outside.

"Takioto."

Yukine seemed overly conscious of Nanami's presence, so I told her to leave us alone for a little bit. Once the maid was out of sight, Yukine turned to me and tried to say something, stammering as she looked for the right words. Her cheeks were slightly flushed.

"Um, so do you really need to flirt with me? Ludie and the captain have their own fan clubs, for one, and they're pretty. I get why you'd do that with President Monica, too. But hitting on me's not really... I mean, just look at me..."

Oh, that's all she's worried about, I thought, unconsciously letting out a sigh.

"Please, Yukine, what are you talking about? I'd be here until the heat death of the universe if I had to list all your charms."

"How do you even have that many compliments?!"

Why wasn't anyone trying to hit on Yukine for real? Why didn't she have her own fan club? She was the loveliest girl around. But I guess you couldn't expect that much from eroge. Hang on, wasn't there someone who looked up to her?

"Well, I may have been exaggerating a little, but I was serious for about ninety-nine percent of it."

"So basically all of it, then?"

"I look forward to working together, Yukine."

"Welcome to the Newspaper Club! I've been waiting for you, Takky ★!"

I had said good-bye to Yukine and was now at the Newspaper Club. I'd planned on coming to campus to take care of something else today, so I had them reschedule their interview with me for today, too.

I failed to repress a sigh at Ivy's hyperactivity and the nickname she had ready for me right from the get-go.

Totally ignoring my initial reaction, the rabbitfolk girl flashed a peace sign right under her eye. Nanami responded with a peace sign in the same spot, as if in retaliation. The two seemed to be enjoying themselves, but what the hell kind of greeting was this?

"Nanami, you don't have to compete with her or anything..."

"C'mon, Takky, what're you talking about ★?! Nanamin and I are best buds, aren't we ♪?"

"I'll ask that you not to refer to me so casually, you cotton-tailed buffoon."

Huh? Weren't you both chatting away a second ago? Where did this swerve come from? Whatever had happened, Ivy was still all smiles.

"Yiiikes, Nanamin's scaaaary! Hippity-hop!"

Uh-oh. Ivy's energy was going to drag me under at this rate.

"…Not to rush things, but could we get to main event here?"

"Fine, if we *haaave* to. I'm all ready for action. *Perfecto!*"

Did she have a condition that forced her to punctuate everything with a pose, or…?

Also, this *Takky* nickname seemed to be set in stone, didn't it?

"All righty then, how about we dive right into the interview? Go ahead and lay it all bare! I'll be sure to edit in a toooon of extra flourishes afterward."

"So you're going to exaggerate everything…"

"It'll be a bigger hit that way, silly! Why don't you start by introducing yourself?"

"Everything's pretty much the same as the news bulletin the Newspaper Club already put out. I'm Assistant Vice-Minister Takioto Kousuke. I guess I'm also technically a member of the Hanamura family, too."

"Yeah, yeah, that's totally fine. Thank youuu! I mean, this intro and whatever are all pretty boilerplate, right? Okay, let's get to the Three Committees stuff next!"

She just kept going and going, didn't she?

"So how did it feel to be appointed as the assistant vice-minister of the Ceremonial Committee? Oh, by the way, I'll probably talk with Minister Benito later about our interview and change it all, okay?"

"Then what's the point of interviewing me in the first place?"

"It'll all be based on your own words, Takky! But we'll change things up whenever we think they could use a bit of a look-over to suit the Ceremonial Committee's purposes. I'll be sure to let you know when we do alter something, though!"

Perhaps Ivy was right about everything I said needing to be run through a Ceremonial Committee filter. The readers were going to bring their own biases to the article anyway. Figuring it was better to have someone go through and scrutinize everything I said instead of just publishing whatever weird nonsense came out of my mouth, I decided to leave things in their hands.

All right, time for a real Ceremonial Committee–style answer.

"Okay, I'll leave the editing up to you. Hmm, if I'm going to play to type, I'd say something like *It's a great honor to etch my name into the annals of the historic Ceremonial Committee. But was there really any doubt I'd be chosen?* How's that sound?"

"Yeah, yeah, that's got a nice Ceremonial Committee ring to it! You're one in a million, Takky. Giving me answers like that is a huuuuuge help. It'll cut down on a lot of editing later!" Ivy said before shifting her eyes down to the documents in front of her.

"All right, then next is…your dungeon-clear story! Ta-daaa! You set a crazy record, clearing the first forty floors all by yourself. Do you have any thoughts on that, Takky?"

"*What's the big deal about it?* …Hmm, a response like that would give President Monica a real headache, right? But if I'm gonna give a faithful Ceremonial Committee answer, that's how it'll sound."

If I riled the students up too much, were they going to try to attempt the same without the skills to back it up?

"Aaah, good point… That might make the Student Council and Morals Committee pull their hair out. Hmmm, but anything you say'll add fuel to the fire, won't it? It's a fun answer, though, so let's get Moni's permission on it before going to print… All righty!" Ivy said, jotting down a note for herself. *Moni* was a real cute nickname.

"Okay, next question! Drumrooooooooll! What's your type? Omigooosh!"

Ivy put both hands up to her cheeks and wiggled back and forth.

As it occurred to me that this question would foreshadow my plans to hit on the Three Committees members, I felt a stare from beside me and turned to meet it.

There stood Nanami, pleading with her eyes to leave the question up to her.

Ignoring the pit forming in my stomach, I decided to let her handle it.

"Miss Ivy, my Master is a bit embarrassed to say this, so while it may be presumptuous of me, I will answer in his stead. He likes silver hair. Preferably cut short."

I snapped my gaze to her the instant I heard that uncannily familiar-sounding description. But Nanami didn't so much as flinch.

"He's charmed by people who have cold, somewhat aloof stares. As it happens, his favorite eye color would be a purplish-red and bluish-purple heterochromia combo. He also prefers outfits that accentuate women's thighs, specifically maid uniforms. Nanami would be his type."

"I was about to cut in with a *You're describing yourself, aren't you?!* but you just came out and said it anyway! I won't deny it, though."

Silver hair on a maid? Phew, boy, what a fantastic combination. Hold on…Nanami? Am I hallucinating, or did you just press up against me?

"Look at you two, that rapport of yours has got me jealous… But do you mind if I mix that up a bit? To be honest, I was planning on changing your answer no matter what since I already had a response in mind."

So what was the point in asking me in the first place?

"Change it how?"

"I want you to respond with Ludie's traits to make it sound like she's your type."

"Fine by me. That should push things in a good direction for my future activities anyway. President Monica would work, too, right? I'll leave the choice on who up to you."

"Yup, yup! I'm glad you pick up on these things so quick! I'll be sure to get everyone's permission. Neeeext question!"

I gave my best Ceremonial Committee–style answers to several more questions, and the interview wrapped up. Then we immediately got to chatting.

"Sheesh, the Three Committees are aaaalways snatching up the best students. Though, we had a *really* good student join us last year, and they've been a humongous help!"

"The Three Committees are very appealing, aren't they?"

"Seriously! They boost your resume a ton when you go look for a job after school, too! The Newspaper Club's no slouch in that department… but we're still no match for the Three Committees, that's for sure! It's enough to make a girl jealous!"

"But you had the skills to join the Three Committees if you wanted, right, Ivy?"

My comment sent a twinkle of suspicion flashing through her eyes.

"Oh, reeeeally? You think so?"

"Sure do."

At the very least, her abilities came within spitting distance of the main heroines. Though, that was mainly because she had access to the ninja class.

"*Tee-hee*, thanks! Speaking of the Three Committees, are you feeling at home yet, Takky? They're pretty uptight about controlling information and all, right? There's gotta be stuff that they haven't told you yet, too. Have they maaaybe gotten up to something that makes you want to join us instead?"

"I'm not thinking about quitting the Ceremonial Committee."

"Really? Awww, too bad! Okay, it's fine if you want to stay in the Ceremonial Committee, but do you have any interest in journalism?"

"That's also gonna be a 'no' from me."

"Figures," Ivy said with a sigh. "*Gaaah*, I still haven't found a first-year who really stands out above the rest. If you know of anyone who's a good match, do you think you could introduce me?!"

There was one person who might fit the bill, but I hadn't even talked to them yet.

As Ivy mulled over what she was going to do, she abruptly struck her fist in her palm.

"Oh, right! Takky, Takky! Talking about a standout first-year reminded me! Do you know him?"

"Know who?"

"He's not on your level, but he is a first-year who everyone has their eye on—Iori Hijiri!"

"What about him?"

"You probably haven't heard about yesterday, right?" Ivy asked, peering intently into my face.

"I haven't, no."

"Well, well, well. Then I'll let you in on it! His party? They made it past the thirtieth layer of the Tsukuyomi Dungeon!"

"Huh..."

I couldn't hold back my grin. I had thought it would've taken them a bit longer. Iori may not have been working with the same knowledge pool as I was, but as far as layers went, he was snapping at my heels already.

In fact, Iori was smack-dab in the middle of his first growth period. I wouldn't be surprised if someone told me he passed layer forty a few days from now.

"What's wrong, Takky? Ohhh, are you getting nervous?"

"I'm not worried at all. Heck, I'm happy to hear it."

"Huh? Happy? Really?"

"Master is a hopeless masochist."

"What're you talking about, Nanami?"

Despite my quip, I couldn't deny her accusation.

"Just hearing that my friend's working hard and putting up the results to show it is enough to make me happy. Well that, and…"

"And…?"

"…no matter who I have to face, I'll take them out and come out on top."

Across my playthroughs, which of the characters had done the most for me?

If I considered this question from every angle, it would have to be Yukine. Everything about her was a slam dunk in my eyes, and she always ranked near the top of my most-used characters since she was strong enough to be one of the Big Three.

From a dungeon-clearing perspective, Nanami ranked quite high as well.

The versatility of her abilities was on par with those of the protagonist, Iori Hijiri, so you could clear any dungeon as long as you built the two of them right. Nanami also made farming loot and materials a breeze.

Romantically speaking, Ludie ranked very high on the list. There weren't many out there who could resist a girl so perfectly designed to capture men's hearts.

But in terms of who I owed the most erotically, only one woman fit the bill.

Ludie and I met up after class and headed over to her laboratory. In a sense, this lady was the most eccentric and unpredictable character in all of *MX*, so I was a bit nervous. However, this was our first time meeting in this world. She wouldn't do anything *too* weird, right?

"It looks like Laboratory I is this way," Nanami said, consulting her Tsukuyomi Traveler. This part of the building was bright and clear, but we hadn't come across anyone else here. Maybe no one wanted to get near her?

After passing through a number of automatic doors, we finally arrived at our destination.

There, we found the woman we'd come here for. A bespectacled woman, a full-body aromatherapy woman, a dark-elf woman—the Ceremonial Committee magistrate, aka Sexy Scientist.

"I've been waiting for you, Takioto, and Your Highness, Princess Ludivine. I'm the Ceremonial Committee magistrate, Anemone de la Cerda. Oh, but I hate my surname, so Anemone's fine," she said with a grin.

Anemone was a dark elf with a huge following of hardcore fans. If I had to guess, I'd say she was as tall as Claris, maybe even taller. But unlike Ludie's maid, who was slender and svelte, Sexy Scientist was quite well-endowed.

"Nice to meet you. I'm Kousuke Takioto, Ceremonial Committee assistant vice-minister."

"...I'm Ludivine, here on the orders of the Morals Committee vice president. It's a pleasure to see you again."

"I am Master Kousuke's stunningly beautiful maid, Nanami."

"Yes, I've wanted to meet you, my cute little lamb. I've been hearing about you and Nanami for quite some time now. And I believe it has been over ten years since we've last seen each other, Your Highness. You've grown quite beautiful."

"Oh, please, Miss Anemone, you're just as lovely yourself."

While Anemone was definitely attractive, I felt that the word *bewitching* or *alluring* was a better fit.

"*Hee-hee.* Now, now, no need to be so formal with me. Same goes for you, little lamb, okay?"

"Okay, *Anemone* it is, then. Anyways, you've got quite the lineup of visitors today, don't you?"

I looked behind and saw a bespectacled girl, along with a silent pink-haired teacher who was hiding potato chips behind her back and averting her gaze.

"Hello, Takioto, Princess Ludivine, Nanami."

Vice President Fran smiled as she pushed her glasses up.

"...Hi," Ms. Ruija said, still avoiding looking me in the eye for some reason.

Sexy Scientist and Ms. Ruija. Nothing good could come from that combo. I decided to pretend I hadn't seen anything. But that was going to be impossible, wasn't it?

"What brings you here, Vice President Fran?"

"I've come to pick up an item the Student Council requested.

Magistrate Anemone makes truly wonderful things for us. Though, she does hand over weird stuff we don't ask for every once in a while."

We eroge players, on the other hand, actually wanted those strange items. In fact, we *requested* that she make them.

"Hold on, what's 'weird' supposed to mean? They're all fantastic, aren't they? By the way, you three seem concerned with Ms. Ruija here. It's a long story."

"Ugh…"

I didn't know why, but I felt nothing but trepidatious about this. Ludie understood my position and gave a strained smile after seeing the looks of distaste Nanami and I wore. From the way Anemone was grinning, I gathered that she must be privy to my relationship with Ms. Ruija, too. Meanwhile, the only person unaware of the current situation, Vice President Fran, cocked her head in confusion.

A groan escaped my lips, and Ms. Ruija hastily shot Nanami a look of annoyance. I stared at the two women, the tall Anemone next to the tiny Ms. Ruija, wondering who was supposed to be the educator between the two.

"Now then, I came here to take care of a few things," I said.

I glanced at Ludie. She nodded, then told Anemone she would handle the situation on her end before handing her a bag.

"This is from the Morals Committee."

"Ah, so it came in. With this, I'll *finally* be able to make it. Thank you!"

"By the way, what exactly will you be creating?" Ludie asked, likely inquiring out of sheer curiosity more than anything else.

"Oh, this? *Tee-hee.* I need the tool you gave me to make a tentacle bomb that will restrain and bind a woman. Aren't you just thrilled at the thought?"

....

Yikes, a gargantuan one right out the gate. What were we supposed to do about this awkwardness, huh? Totally inappropriate for a first encounter. Not nearly enough time had passed since meeting Anemone for a comment like that, right?

I wish she would have gone from zero to one instead of zero to one hundred on the weirdo scale, at the very least. Look, Ludie's totally at a loss for words. Though Ms. Ruija and Vice President Fran had to be used to it by now, seeing as they were just glaring at her with disgust.

"Hey, Kousuke. Was I carrying tentacles this whole time...?"

Ludie looked rattled. I bet Yukine didn't know the truth, either. If she had, she would've brought it here herself to ensure no harm befell anyone.

But *tentacles*, huh? Despite my incredible, extreme, astounding levels of curiosity, I decided not to pry any further. Everyone else had a terrifying look in her eyes. That being said, I would have to consider purchasing the device from Anemone on the down-low once this was over.

"Well, what do you say? Interested?" Anemone asked.

Naturally, I was *very* interested. But why were you sending the conversation my way while I was trying so hard to play it all off like it was nothing? Anemone was definitely doing it on purpose. Please don't look at me with that beaming smile on your face.

"What a fantastic item indeed. It would suit you perfectly, Master."

I would've liked to interrogate Nanami for an hour or so to really dig into what exactly about it "fit me perfectly."

"...Spare me the stupid jokes and let's get on with it, okay?"

But I wasn't going to deny that I *did* want it, and I wouldn't have minded providing developmental support if necessary.

"Now then, what did you need my help with, little lamb?"

"Ah, right."

Anemone's revelation had been so impactful that I'd almost forgotten why I came here in the first place.

"Actually, there's something I'd really like you to make for me."

"Oh, something for you personally, is it?"

In *Magical★Explorer*, you can develop items once you gain access to any of the three laboratories. The fastest way to unlock them is joining one of the Three Committees. Then you can place a few characters in the lab and have them craft items for you. On some occasions, their creations are required to obtain characters' ultimate weapons.

On top of that system, you can also pay Anemone or the teachers with money or items to have them make you things in return. That was what I was after this time.

"Yeah, an item for capturing angels and demons. And I'll need quite a lot of them," I said, prompting Nanami to poke me. I turned and saw that she had placed a hand on her cheek and was bashfully shaking her head.

"Honestly, Master, you could have just told me… I'm always ready and waiting for you ♪!"

Uh, what the hell is going through your head?! No way am I planning to use them on you! And now I'm embarrassed just imagining it, so knock it off!

"So that's what you had in mind… I'm raring to go all of a sudden!"

"Can we cut this off here? I'm getting some downright arctic stares. The items are just for going into the dungeon, okay?"

"Oh my, dungeon role-play…?"

"Dungeon role-play, Master…? That will earn you seven billion and three hundred million Respect Points."

Please don't whisper weird stuff like that! I can feel the glares stabbing right through me here. The vice president's scowl is *especially* scary. And that's way too many damn points!

"Putting the jokes aside for now, I will craft these items for you under one condition."

"A condition?"

"Yes. There's something I want for another item I'm looking to produce. I want you to get it for me. Oh, but if you're in a rush, then I'll give you priority. Anyone capable of joining the Ceremonial Committee can be trusted enough to get me what I need."

"Thank you very much. In that case, could you work on my items first?"

"Very well, then let's get down to business. Can you give me a detailed explanation of what you're aiming to use these on? Also, I'll need magic sigil stones to make them, along with a few other things I can't do without…"

"Oh, that stuff." I nodded. "I've already gotten together a few things I thought you might need. I have several sigil stones with me, and I can bring even more if need be."

Nanami produced a bag after I said that. The truth was that she'd actually gathered them all herself while I was in the library or elsewhere. Anemone took the bag and stared at me, impressed.

"…Oh my."

I could tell that Anemone's gaze had sharpened. From what I understood, this expression of hers signified that she'd taken an interest in what was in front of her.

"How did you know what I would need?"

The looks in Ms. Ruija's and Vice President Fran's eyes also changed when they heard Anemone's question.

"I haven't gotten anything mixed up, have I? I'll tell you all about it later on, promise."

"*Hee-hee*, then we'll need to discuss specifications right away. Fran, Ms. Ruija. If you're done here, then make yourselves scarce."

Then I chimed in. "Oh, Ms. Ruija, I also have something I'd like to talk with you about. Until then. Actually, hang on, you said you also have some business here, right?"

I needed to press her about what she'd come here to do. Just in case. I prayed that Anemone wasn't getting a new machine ready. She smiled at my question.

"Oh, little lamb. You needn't worry about Ms. Ruija too much."

"Huh? What do you mean?"

"Because she's been coming here to look into your physical constitution."

"M-Ms. Ruija?" I asked, flabbergasted.

The instructor smiled sheepishly before responding:

"Well, the truth is…I'm still worried, is all. But the thing is, we haven't found anything out, so…I thought it would be better not to mention anything."

"M-Ms. Ruija…!"

"You have a wonderful teacher looking out for you, don't you, little lamb?"

"I really do."

It meant a lot that she was investigating things for me.

"Ahh, yes," Anemone said, clapping her hands. "That's right, she also drops by for some snacks occasionally. She's actually made off with quite a lot of them, and it's put me in a real bind. I hear her allowance is quite small."

I turned to Ms. Ruija, who went bright red and shot her eyes down to the floor.

After finishing my discussion with Anemone and parting ways with Ludie, Nanami and I looked for a place to talk with Ms. Ruija.

It seemed like she didn't want anyone to overhear what she had to say, so we sat down on a deserted bench. After getting our instructor settled, Nanami and I went over to a vending machine, where I purchased the milk tea that Ms. Ruija often liked to drink.

"Do you want anything, Nanami?"

"Master's sweat woul—"

"Got it, milk tea for you, too," I interjected, buying the same beverage as I had for Ms. Ruija. I decided I was also fine with that and ultimately got three of them. Ms. Ruija was off in her own world on the bench, looking deep in thought, but she thanked me when I passed her a can.

I looked at her and sighed as she gazed out across Tsukuyomi Magic Academy's vast premises.

Ms. Ruija was very popular among a subset of eroge players, myself included. Her adorable design had the endearing qualities of a small defenseless animal; it was impossible to not want to protect her. Plus, she smelled like she'd been standing in a field of flowers, though I was pretty sure that was just the scent of her shampoo. Oh, and her boobs were huge. However, she was also debt-ridden and totally gullible.

"There's something I wanted to talk to you about," Ms. Ruija said. Before all this, I would have chuckled with glee at the prospect of being approached by a beautiful teacher for a chat, but at this point, I could only feel dread at the thought of the bomb she was going to drop on me next.

For the time being, I decided to play dumb to avoid whatever was coming.

"You want me to increase your allowance, right? Sure."

"R-really?! Whoo-hoo, all ri— No, wait, that's not what I mean!"

"Oh? Okay, then we'll keep it the same."

Hearing this, Ms. Ruija started stammering "abuh, abuh, abuh," looking truly flustered. This must have been the first time I'd ever seen someone stutter like an exaggerated cartoon character in real life before.

"Ah, no, that's not it! I wanted to talk about something else!" she insisted.

I tried desperately to shake her off as she latched on to me, squinting her eyes in distress. I was just joking, of course.

"Okay, sure, I get it, I get it. So then why did you actually pull me aside?"

"Oh, right. While I was going over the information I looked into during Yuika's kidnapping, something stood out to me as a bit strange. Then I investigated further, and well…it's *very* suspicious."

"Are you sure it's all right to show us this?"

"Yes. I thought it over and figured I should come to you with this, Takioto."

Ms. Ruija took out several documents, giving a reminder while doing so. "This is personal information, so don't talk about it to anyone else okay?"

"Uhhh…what is this?"

A list of workers?

"When I saw this, I thought…*this is an awfully small number.*"

"Of workers?"

"That's right. And doesn't it seem like the employees have been working there an unusually long time? I've never even seen a few of these names before."

Things were starting to smell fishy. Was there a chance that this had anything to do with the Church of the Malevolent Lord?

"…Have you checked in with Marino about all this? Also, why are you sharing this secret information with the two of us?"

I carefully read over the list of names. There were librarians, clerks, systems engineers, and various others. I understood why one of these names was on the list. She was still making her preparations, so I wasn't worried there, but I was in the dark about the rest of the people.

"I thought about it. But Nanami said that I should always talk things over with her first in the event that anything happens, so…"

I turned around.

"Getting dirt on you was the correct call, then," Nanami said.

"But you promised you wouldn't say anything about it!" cried Ms. Ruija.

If Nanami had the information, she wasn't going to do anything untoward, so Ms. Ruija was probably fine. Wait, scratch that. There *was* a chance of something happening.

"What the hell are you two up to…?"

"*Ahem*, that wasn't the only reason. The principal knows a few of the people on this list very well, so I thought she might try to dodge the question."

True, there was certainly a chance she would avoid the topic. She had done the same when I asked her about Yuika, too.

"By the way, I made sure to impress upon Ms. Ruija that she needs to run anything involving Marino by me first."

"That's right. Which is why I thought I'd come to both you and Nanami, since you also seem to know a lot, Takioto. I plan on bringing this to the principal after our conversation, of course!"

"I sorta get the situation. But what if I was Marino's accomplice and hadn't said anything, or I was working against you and confiscated these documents? What would you do then?"

"Oh... Um, well, um, you helped me out, didn't you? I—I sorta figured you wouldn't use this information for anything bad, so..."

"...That's fine, I suppose. Thank you."

"Weeeeeh."

I teased Ms. Ruija before we skimmed through the documents she had prepared for us. Sure enough, there were many areas that struck me as strange. As I thought this over, Ms. Ruija pointed to a woman's name.

"...Oh, I know her very well, and I run into her quite often. But look... apparently, she's been working at the Academy since before I was even a student here."

Staring at the name, Nanami cocked her head.

"Now that I think about it, I don't believe I've met her yet. You often go to see her, Master, but I do not."

That was because I was making sure they wouldn't cross paths to avoid any close calls.

"I'm sure it's just some racial trait of hers, but she hasn't changed in the slightest after all these years... I'm a little bit envious," Ms. Ruija remarked.

"Is that so? That makes me slightly curious," Nanami said.

"Don't worry, Nanami. You'll meet in due time. Won't be long until all chips are on the board," I reassured her.

Once everything with Gabby is settled, I'll have everything in place, I thought. Then I would leap into action. Tackle the most dangerous and difficult event yet. An event that would be very important when thinking to the future.

I hadn't said anything about it to Nanami. I couldn't. Thus, her current look of confusion was only to be expected.

In front of our eyes was a file, complete with a smiling picture, on librarian Rue Sakura.

"*Mmmm*, delicious ☆! Thank youuuu, Takioto!"

She made it look so very tasty. I couldn't help smiling myself.

Nanami had some more business with Ms. Ruija, so I parted ways with her and had just finished meeting back up with Yuika following her visit to the Ceremonial Committee. From there, we hit up a modern Wakoku-style café nearby, and she had been eating cake ever since.

Honestly, I wanted to feed her all the cake she wanted.

"Are you really okay with treating me to this?"

"Don't worry about it. The stuff with Gabby—er, Gabriella is a headache for you, too. Speaking of, why did you go off in my defense when you first met her? I was happy to hear it, obviously, but now you're totally in her crosshairs, right?"

Anyone familiar with Yuika Hijiri would have been shocked to see the shouting match she'd had with Gabby.

In *Magical★Explorer*, the character of Yuika Hijiri is a worldly girl who leverages her charm and attractiveness to build relationships.

When she joins the Student Council or the Morals Committee, she cleverly flaunts her charms to endear herself to both classmates and upperclassmen alike.

If she chooses the Ceremonial Committee, she instead cozies up to the powerful members of the Three Committees, making it appear as though she's bribing instructors (who are actually collaborating with the Ceremonial Committee, of course) to attract the ire of the student body.

Seeing as she was well-liked by the upperclassmen of the Three Committees, it was safe to say that she possessed an exceptional ability to endear herself to others.

The way she flaunted her charms wasn't unintentional, of course, but a skill she had cultivated. This was where her near-perfect fake smile had arisen from.

I mean, Yuika herself would even say stuff like *Winsomeness is a weapon that can fell even fearsome foes with ease.* Who did she think she was, Natsume Sōseki?

Yuika was a powerful main heroine, though, so she could wield exceptional strength in-game, even putting her charm to work.

"Hmmm, good question…," she said before averting her gaze and scratching the back of her head with a bashful smile on her face.

"I don't really understand it myself. I seriously thought I'd just fade away into the background. I didn't care about whatever she said to me…or I didn't before. But when I saw your face and then looked at Evangelista laughing it up, um, how do I put it? I don't really get it, either, but the blood just sorta *fwoosh*ed up to my head!"

I had assumed Yuika would just fade away, too.

It wouldn't have been strange to see the game version of Yuika just say, *Okay, laters ☆!* and leave the area. Yet instead, she'd butted in.

"*Ah-ha-ha*…," Yuika laughed, scratching her cheek. "But seriously, I wonder why? You don't really, like, get other people to want to protect you or anything."

"You just sneaked a jab at me, didn't you?"

"Not at all. You're super reliable, and *that's* why you don't arouse any protective instincts in people. Especially after everything that's happened lately."

What the hell was with this girl, casually tearing me down before building me right back up? She was a little too good at scoring points with me, wasn't she?

That said, while I did enjoy supporting other people, I wouldn't say no to having people pamper and dote on me, too.

Yuika's fork hand abruptly came to a stop on top of the table. Then, averting her gaze, she mumbled:

"…But anyway, Evangelista leaves quite the impression, doesn't she?"

No question about it, she was quite a striking girl. However…

"She's memorable, sure, but you can't be shocked by everyone like her who shows up."

There were many other characters on a similar level to Gabby.

Besides, Gabby still hadn't actually demonstrated her real power yet.

She stood out the most not in her current state, but after she joined the Ceremonial Committee. That was because she abandoned her uniform and started wearing a dress all the time at that point.

Once she did, the ostentatiousness of her getup rivaled Shion's for the title of gaudiest student in school.

The presentation of Shion's Wakoku-style outfit and Gabby's dress made them the two largest presences in the Ceremonial Committee.

"Seriously…? What's with this academy of weirdos anyway…? There's already plenty of oddballs as is," said Yuika.

"Yeah, I suppose there's Orange, and Shion, and Sis, and Nanami."

Ms. Ruija and Ivy, too. Save for Minister Benito, the whole Ceremonial Committee classified as weirdos.

"There's also you and Yukine."

"…Whoa, whoa, whoa. Slow down a minute. You're lumping *me* in with them?"

"Um, I don't know how to break it to you, but I'm pretty sure you're a top-class weirdo, even if you take Nanami out of the picture."

"What?!"

"Uhh… Personally, I can't believe you're even reacting like that," she said, reaching out for my stole. "Not that it really matters."

"It *definitely* matters," I protested.

"So what's Evangelista like anyway? If you know anything, I'm all ears."

Totally brushing me off, huh?

"You picked a fight while being totally in the dark about her?"

"I didn't pick the fight. I just felt obligated to join in on the fight she was picking with you and back you up! You should be thanking me for taking up the gauntlet instead!"

"Right, sure, sure. Thanks. Eat as much as you'd like."

"And I will gladly take you up on the delicious offer. Thaaaaaank you. Though, I still feel you could be a biiiiiit more grateful, so how about we compromise here, and I'll settle for you gifting me a luxury apartment instead?"

I knew she was just joking, but I did technically own an apartment building. I even had Ms. Ruija living there right now. I wondered how Yuika would react if I really did grant her wish.

"Oh, sure, I'll get you one when the mood strikes. Getting back on topic, though, Gabriella's the little sister of Minister Benito, who's like the president of the Ceremonial Committee. If you took away my dungeon score on the last test, she would be the top of the class. She's technically Leggenze royalty, too."

That wasn't so special when you considered that President Monica and Shion were also royalty, albeit of different countries.

"Huh...," she replied with disinterest before taking a bite of cheesecake. "Yum!"

"...You're looking real optimistic for someone who'll be squaring off against her soon. Lose, and it's your head that'll roll, you know."

"First of all, there's no way you're going to lose, and I don't really see myself losing to someone like her, either. It's more that...well...is she really going to drop out of school?"

In spite of what Yuika may have felt about Gabby, she was genuinely worried for her after all.

"It'll be fine, don't worry. Even if I win, I'm not gonna let her quit school."

"You're going to make her do something lewd instead, right?"

"Like hell I am, stupid! But forget that. What do you mean that you don't see yourself losing to her? You don't even know that much about her, right?"

Unfortunately for Gabby, I didn't think Yuika was going to lose, either. However, I could only say that with my experience playing the game, so I was curious how Yuika could arrive at the same conclusion when she hadn't even heard Gabby's name before.

"Ah, how do I put it? Let's see. Hmm, I guess you could say that I have, like, killer intuition."

"What's that supposed to mean?"

"I don't know how to explain it, but it sorta feels like I'm able to get a sense of someone's abilities. Evangelista doesn't really set off any alarm bells for me."

This was an effect of Yuika's Sense Danger skill.

It's an extremely helpful ability that both raises certain stats and increases the likelihood of escaping an encounter with an opponent that's stronger (i.e. higher level) than the user.

The boosted escape rate it affords is so critical to speedrunning that I doubt there's anyone who doesn't use it to shorten their runs.

Depending on Iori's choices, you can also add Yuika to the party before your first exams, too.

"What do you mean?"

Of course, Yuika hadn't personally told me about her skill yet, so I pretended to be none the wiser and asked for more clarification.

"Just that Evangelista probably isn't that great in combat, really. Sure, she's in the top of the class if you look at her test scores or whatever, but it feels like ranking based on exam results doesn't really tell you much. I've seen a whole lot of people who seem much more dangerous than her already."

"Yeah, studying and fighting are totally different. Our deepest dungeon level is also going to be taken into account on our next test, so I think things will start to look different then. Wait, but who are these other 'dangerous people' supposed to be?"

People who seemed dangerous to the girl with the Sense Danger skill? Now, that was intriguing.

"Well, there's Katou for one, and Ludivine, too. There's also the foxfolk student who takes naps on benches. Oh, and you're included in that group as well, Takioto. Heck, you're at the top of the pack if anything. And while I wouldn't say he'd give you a run for your money or anything…my big brother has surprised me in more ways than one."

I thought back to that moment. The things he said to me.

If I had to guess, Iori was powering up right this very moment.

"Iori, huh… Can't let him catch me off guard."

"I didn't want to lose to him, either, to be honest."

I was taken aback for a moment at the revelation.

"…You're kidding, right?"

"Nope, it's true."

"When?"

"Today in class. The one that *someone* didn't show up for."

In the game, there are certain instances when Yuika enters the story with higher stats than Iori. Some new players even end up losing to her. But obviously, the latent mass of potential that is Iori goes on to surpass Yuika. Depending on how you build him, he can even beat her early on a first-time playthrough.

"Really stressing my faults, aren't you?" I said.

Now then, what about in this current situation?

Yuika had gained a lot of experience points in her previous dungeon visit.

But if Iori was still able to best her, then it could only mean that he was steadily strengthening himself as well.

"What sort of fight was it?"

"I mean, the match had all sorts of restrictions and everything, but to cut to the chase, we had a melee fight."

Melee combat is Yuika's specialty. Of course, Iori himself is just as proficient in that area. Honestly, he's capable of doing anything depending on how he's built.

"And it really gave me a lot to think about."

"Did it, now...?"

"How do I put it? My thoughts were all jumbled up and swirling around in my head. But the simplest way to describe it was *frustration*."

"I mean, I can understand that."

Everyone felt frustration when they lost. The only exceptions were those who weren't that devoted to victory in the first place, the types who truly had no interest in competition.

"I've actually never lost to my brother before this. So I thought I'd continue to beat him from here on out forever. I know my Iori aaaaall too well. But."

"But?"

"It was that look of his. He was almost like a different person, like a dragon had come down and possessed him or something."

"Huh?"

"My big brother stopped being the person I knew. But he was still himself."

"Very philosophical."

"I know, even I feel like I'm not making sense here."

"But I get what you're trying to say."

Oh, I got it. I understood her *very* well.

"Really? You're not lying to me, are you? Anyway...the reason he changed is he set a big goal for himself."

A goal, was it?

"That's what he told you?"

"Yup, but he said he was too embarrassed to tell me what it was exactly."

I imagined that one of his motives had to do with Yuika, so he probably couldn't bring himself to admit it in front of her.

"I think maybe that's why I lost," she said, staring into the air.

Then a self-deprecating smile came to her face, and she stood up.

Yuika stretched up to the sky and spun around in place, puffing out her chest and holding her arms out wide.

"See, look, I'm really light, aren't I?"

She wasn't talking about her body weight here, of course.

"Yeah, you're suuuuuuuper flimsy."

"Yiiikes, that's awful. Don't you know how to sugarcoat comments like that? That's really harsh. You're better off waiting until your next life if you're trying to be an emotionally attractive guy, too. No way you're getting a girlfriend like that."

"Oh, shut up, you're also being mean! I *do* want to become a hottie, both inside and out. Besides, I can totally sugarcoat comments! When the time and place call for it!"

"…Anyway, I might not be wafer-thin, but I'll go ahead and admit that I'm flimsy and weak. I was thinking maybe that's why I lost."

Yuika fell silent.

"The truth is, everyone's like that. Even the most impressive adults have parts of themselves that are flimsy and hollow. Some even manage some level of success despite that, but it's just…," I said.

"Just what?"

"Those aren't the sort of people who end up accomplishing something really, really big, are they? I think strength is sort of the same way."

"I think so, too."

"That's why I think I lost to my big brother," she quietly murmured.

"So then how do you want to end up, Yuika?"

"Me? I've basically always thought a life where I can have fun is good enough for me ★!'"

"That sounds like something you'd say."

"But it's suuuuuuuuuuuper frustrating, though."

"Is that all? Frustration? You don't have other goals or anything?"

"Does it look like I do?"

"Hey, I don't know… Like getting married or something?"

"Excuuuse me? I'm not in elementary school anymore, so could you bring a more mature dream to the table? That's got nothing to do with this conversation, does it?"

"Well, the bride thing was a joke, but the way I see it, you have the potential to become anything you want to be."

Yuika had amazing people skills, smarts, and above all else, grit.

"I definitely can't become *anything*, and I don't even want to, either. I do think it'd be nice to have the strength to protect myself, though."

"That's a shame."

"What is?"

"I was thinking that with your potential, you could aim to reach the same level as President Monica."

"Uhhhh? You need to look at reality, please. R-E-A-L-I-T-Y!"

"I'm being serious. On top of that, I think even Iori will climb to those heights, too."

Yuika shot me a glare.

After really letting her eyes bore into mine, she released a sigh.

"I don't have any goals, but I do want to avoid being a burden to people..."

"Being a burden?"

"I've burdened so many people throughout my life, from Iori to my parents, and made them worry. Do you know how much that hurts?"

I guess I sort of saw where she was coming from. During my forty-layer solo dungeon clear, it was hard knowing that I was making so many people anxious.

"Part of it is that I want to become strong enough that I won't cause people any more trouble than I already have... Though, the biggest reason is that I just don't want to lose."

"Don't you think that's enough?"

"What do you mean?"

"Enough of a reason to grow stronger, I mean. You don't want to burden people, Iori included, and you don't want to lose."

"...Is that really enough of a reason?"

"Sure it is. But it's fine to cause trouble for other people, okay?" I said, pointing at myself. "Like for me."

"Oh, I mean, that goes without saying, doesn't it? I'm going to rely on you with every fiber of my being."

"Bring it on. But you'll come help me out when I'm in trouble, too, right?"

"Please, Takioto, do you even need to ask? The answer's obvious. Rest assured, I definitely won't be coming to your aid!"

"Why the hell not?!"

"*Hee-hee-hee.* I'm going to make you work yourself to the bone, so I hope you're ready!"

Yuika had been little down, but it seemed like she had regained some of her pep again.

"…If you really want to get strong and you really do trust me, then why don't we head into a dungeon together?" I asked.

"Hmmm, a dungeon? With *you*?"

Her tone was repulsed, but her expression was pleased.

"Well, I suppose if you insist."

"Where's this patronization coming from…?"

"Ah, not to change the subject, but I told you that I lost to my brother for the first time, right? I actually experienced another first just now."

"And what's that?"

"Oh, no, it's a little bit embarrassing, but…," Yuika said, looking up at me with a bashful smile and upturned eyes.

"…this is the first time I've ever laid out my bare-naked feelings to someone else before!"

She was so cute. And coquettish. Coquettishly cute.

The way she averted her eyes ever so slightly after she finished talking and tilted her head when our eyes met again was just as cute, too.

This was Yuika we were talking about. She was definitely doing this on purpose. Even knowing that, I felt my heart skip a beat.

"This is my first time, so you better be sure to make me strong, okay?"

—Shion's Perspective—

"Minister," I called out, prompting him to slowly turn toward me.

"What is it, Shion?"

"You sicced your little sister on Kou, yes? Did she come complaining to you?"

"Hmm, saying I 'sicced' her on him isn't a very nice way of putting it. I just had a bit of a talk with Gabriella, honest. All I did was praise Takioto."

"You still guided her in that direction, yes? Almost like a con artist."

The minister laughed.

"*Ha-ha-ha.* I do feel bad, but there wasn't anything else I could do for her."

"There wasn't?"

"No. See, from my perspective, Gabriella's overflowing with raw talent."

"That is quite clear, given she's second in her year."

Geniuses flocked to attend Tsukuyomi Academy, so earning a high rank was no easy feat. Yet she'd been able to place top in her class, disregarding Kou's irregular circumstances, despite it all. It wasn't difficult to imagine the talents at her disposal.

"But when I think of Gabriella, it becomes clearer and clearer that I'm a fool."

"And where in heaven's name is this coming from?"

"The thing is, I caged Gabriella in order to protect her."

"You mean to say she had a pampered upbringing?"

"Feel free to interpret it that way—you're basically on the mark. And to keep herself from being threatened, she never left that cage."

"Is that so?"

"Sure is. And because I remained there with her, she never truly left my side."

"I haven't the foggiest idea what you are trying to get at here."

"Sorry, sorry. Simply put, I'm locking away Gabriella's talents. I'm restricting her behavior, too. Positively villainous, don't you think? That's why I think of myself as even more despicable than the students make me out to be."

"Well, there are indeed many on campus who think so. You can say the same for me."

As long as we were part of the Ceremonial Committee, it was unavoidable.

"I talked about Takioto with Gabriella because I thought he could serve as an impetus."

"An impetus, you say? To make her stretch out her wings and leave her cage, you mean?"

"Yup, that's it. People need something to motivate them to take action. It could be your own intellectual curiosity that pushes you. It could be another person. Besides that, well... *Hee-hee*, it could be money, perhaps, or a sense of rivalry that drives you."

"What will you do should she fly out from her cage and plummet? If it turns out letting her free was a mistake?"

"You're awful mean, Shion..."

"I am merely discussing possibilities, as unpleasant as they may be."

The minister lifted his head and looked at me.

"Kou is surely the correct choice. I feel that he shall lead her in the proper direction," Shion said.

"And what's your evidence for that?"

"Why, the intuition I trust, of course."

The minister gawked for a moment before quickly bursting into laughter.

"*Ha-ha*, you're right, I can definitely put my faith in that."

"Mocking me, are you?"

"No, no, not at all. I like it, I'll have to use that myself next time! 'The intuition I trust.'"

"That's my personal catchphrase, you know. Normally, I would charge you to let you use it; however…you, Minister, can have my special permission."

He certainly seemed to be enjoying himself, judging by his smile.

"The truth is that I'm certain Takioto will do a good job. That's why I left it up to him. Things really seem to have gotten out of hand all of a sudden, though."

"Out of hand?"

"If Takioto loses the competition, he has to quit the Ceremonial Committee, and if Gabriella loses, she has to drop out of school… Takioto assured me he wasn't going to let anything like that happen and that he would take care of everything, but…I really do feel bad about pushing this on Takioto… I get the sense that all my hair's going to fall out on me, *ha-ha*."

Despite Benito's chuckle, there was little doubt he was quite worried. Be that as it may, Kou surely had an infinitesimal chance of losing.

"If Kou assured you as such, then I see no problem. All we can do is watch over them."

"…You're right."

"That takes care of that…mostly. There is one more thing I want to say."

"What's that?"

"You disparaged yourself just now, yes? Spouting nonsense about being despicable or what have you."

The minister nodded.

"You should know that Esmeralda, Yukine, Fran, and I all look up to you. The same goes for Kou. Even Monica herself recognizes your abilities."

"Shion…"

"Most importantly, Gabriella idolizes you and aspires to emulate you herself, yes? If you did insist on calling yourself scum, then you are thus debasing everyone who admires you."

I rose to my feet and opened the door.

"You are a true ceremonial minister, understand?"

People with a penchant for speedrunning *MX* almost always make use of a certain item in their endeavor—a chart that outlines their route through the game.

They would refine their route by coming up with ways to increase their efficiency while occasionally referencing the charts of others. Additionally, there's one more thing these speedrunners (myself included) would almost invariably do on their runs—obtain a specific skill.

"A ninja skill...?"

In *Magical★Explorer*, the ninja class gets special treatment.

Thanks to the strength of this job, a male character in the Student Council with access to it outperforms most of the other male characters in the game. It also allows Ivy, the Newspaper Club girl, to stand toe to toe with some of the main heroines in combat.

There are a number of ways to obtain the ninja skill in question. You can either learn it from an instructor or student character well versed in ninjutsu, or you can obtain it in one of the dungeons. Normally, the former would be the quickest route for picking up skills in general.

However, considering that one of the skills I had to acquire at all costs could only be obtained in a dungeon, that I had some chores to take care of, and that I wanted to grab a couple of items in the most efficient manner possible, I thought it best to visit this dungeon instead.

I guess you could say it was practically fate that I ended up coming here.

Still, depending on how I advanced through the dungeon, begging the instructors or other characters to teach me may not have been too bad, either. Of course, that was only true if clearing the dungeon was taking up more time and effort than I wanted.

There was just one skill I couldn't do without. As long as I could get my hands on it, I'd decide how to take care of my other tasks based on my progress. In any case, I didn't have to think about that at the moment.

Instead, I needed to focus on the dungeon in front of me. Or at least, I should have, but…

"…I still can't get over how off this feels."

…I just kept getting distracted.

"What's wrong?"

Ludie looked at me, puzzled.

"I mean, we're walking on tatami with our shoes on," I said, pointing down at our feet.

We were fighting through Karakuri Trick Castle, one of the dungeons that you unlock by either joining the Three Committees or by progressing down to a certain layer of the Tsukuyomi Dungeon.

Karakuri Trick Castle, exactly as the name implied, was a Japanese-style castle dungeon that had traps and unique mechanisms littered about it.

Visually, it sort of resembled the Ōoku inner section of old Edo Castle, which served as the women's quarters.

The walls of the corridors were constructed of paper partitions or sliding doors, so it felt like we were inside an old-style Japanese house.

The possibility that I could break through the flimsy walls crossed my mind, and I tried slamming my fist into one of the paper doors. But while it bent, it never broke. There had to be some strange force protecting them, so it didn't look like we'd be able to make any shortcuts for ourselves. My experiences in dungeons up until now had taught me that anything was possible inside them, so seeing impervious paper sliding screens didn't faze me in the slightest.

This was all well and good, but the real problem was the floor at our feet. I didn't feel anything walking over wooden floors, but tatami was a whole different story. It was hard to place, but the flooring had this unnatural feeling to it, a strange springiness that was akin to stepping on rubber. Plus, the mere fact that I was going across tatami in my outdoor shoes filled me with revulsion.

"It does feel weird, yeah."

As I watched Ludie, Nanami, and Yuika trample over the tatami, a thought suddenly came to me. Was tatami in the perfect position to satisfy one's fetish-filled mind? If I became one of these mats, then the girls could literally step all over me, even smother me with their butts when they sat down.

Uh-oh, now I was the one getting weird here.

As my chest swelled with not-insignificant envy toward the tatami, Nanami smoothly readied her bow. Almost simultaneously, Yukine put her hands on her naginata.

I immediately brandished my stole and placed my palm on my katana before signaling Ludie, a stern expression already coming over her, with a glance.

"Here they come, Master," said Nanami.

A moment later, four-something yokai appeared.

Keeping in line with the name and appearance of Karakuri Trick Castle, they were uniformly Japanese in design.

"Adzukiarai and ittan-momen, huh."

Adzukiarai and ittan-momen were low-level monsters that appeared in the early layers of every Japanese-style dungeon, this one included.

"Leave the flying ones to me," Ludie announced.

After entrusting the ittan-momen to her and Nanami, Yuika and I dashed forward to deal with the adzukiarai.

The annoying thing about adzukiarai was that they possessed long-ranged attacks. Noticing our approach, the creatures began to attack us, firing off magic masses that resembled their namesake—adzuki red beans.

Fortunately, the missiles weren't very fast, so I easily deflected them with my stole.

And I wasn't the only one parrying them.

"Hmm? Is something wrong?"

Yuika deflected the projectile beans with her gauntlet as she looked over at me.

"This is no sweat for you, huh?" I shouted.

I'd gotten a look at Yuika's abilities in the previous dungeon. She did indeed possess a main heroine's strength, so she'd be able to improve by leaps and bounds if she kept training. However, she does have an unfortunate downside in the game: Her role in battle overlaps a bit with St. Doomsday, the Founding Saint.

Still, Yuika is cute in a sort of obnoxious way, her thighs and black knee socks are an exceptional combo, she refers to you as "big brother," and she doesn't overlap in any *other* areas, so saying that I loved her would be putting it mildly. There was no way I *wasn't* going to include her in my party in this world.

Besides, as long as you weren't trying to speedrun, it was fine having two healers to a party at once. She'd have no issues being in the same group as the Founding Saint... If anything, the two of them actually worked really well together. That was partially down to how alien the Founding Saint was, though.

"Oh, c'mon, Takioto, you're not having any trouble, either!" Yuika yelled back.

That may have been true, but I'd only risen to this level by dedicating myself to training alongside everyone else. I'd want to cry myself to sleep if I was still weak after all that.

Anyway, I was surprised that Yuika could move so deftly, given she hadn't collected many magic particles yet. This must've been what talent looked like. They don't call her the most gifted of the first-years in the game for nothing.

"All right, I'm going to send one flying this way. The rest is up to you."

Saying this, I dashed off, barreling forward as I reflected the adzuki missiles flying at me. There were two adzukiarai ahead of me. After I slammed my Fourth Hand down hard on one of their heads, I then grabbed the creature and pitched it back toward Yuika while drawing my katana.

After making sure the other adzukiarai was split clean in two, I turned to Yuika.

"Taaake this!"

A white light was radiating from her gauntlets, either with mana or some skill. She put the weight of her whole body behind her fist and slammed it into the adzukiarai I'd hurled toward her.

"Now that's a knockout punch."

"Hearing you compliment me sounds like you're making fun of me... Honestly, at my current level, I can't imagine myself besting you. Though, I *can* see myself getting cleaved in two."

I couldn't hold back a dry smile as Yuika stared hard in my direction.

I was trying to grow stronger to be the best conceivable version of myself, after all. If I was using all the knowledge at my disposal and still falling short of Yuika, then I would have no hope of catching up to Iori, the Big Three, and the rest of the main heroines.

"You'll get stronger. If you've got the motivation, it's practically guaranteed."

"The question is, how can you say that with such confidence, hmm…?"

Because I knew it as a fact.

"Good job, everyone. That was some fantastic teamwork," Yukine said with a smile, having watched our fight.

I had asked her to accompany us but steer clear of most of the fighting this time. It would be a good experience for Yuika. Naturally, Yukine had agreed to the request.

She finished collecting the magic stones and cotton cloth dropped by the cloth monster, ittan-momen, along with the magic stones from the adzukiarai, before muttering:

"Guess we keep going, then."

"Actually, could you wait a second, Yukine? How's it look, Nanami?"

I signaled the maid with a look.

"Indeed, my Nanami sensor's ringing loud and clear. It should be around here."

I had already planned out this exchange with her beforehand, so I punched the wall hard right after she said that. But there was no reaction. It had to be around here, right? This time, I slammed the opposite side of the corridor.

Thinking maybe it was the section right next to it, I threw another punch into the paper wall. I was rewarded with a loud *ka-shunk*, like something fitting into place, and the wall slowly slid sideways.

A corridor had appeared before us. I would need to go through this hidden path to get my hands on my coveted ninja skill.

"Let's go this way."

"…I have a feeling I'm going to be in your debt again by the end of this," Yukine said with a strained smile as she entered the passageway.

Just before I could follow behind her, someone grabbed my arm and pulled me back.

"W-wait just a second here. W-was that a secret door?! Uh, Takioto, this is supposed to be your first time here, right?! Better yet, why are you all so chill about a freaking hidden door showing up out of nowhere?!"

It was Yuika who'd grabbed me. I was ready to give the explanation I had prepared ahead of time, but Ludie answered in my stead.

"You're better off not worrying about it. There's no telling what sort of nonsense Kousuke will pull next." She continued addressing Yuika as she followed Yukine down the secret path. "I mean, he soloed forty layers of the Tsukuyomi Academy Dungeon before this, and he also knew the secrets of the Beginner's Dungeon."

Nanami addressed Yuika as she stood in front of the door, dumbfounded.

"Let's go, Miss Yuika."

Yuika looked entirely unconvinced, but she ultimately didn't say anything more and started down the hidden path.

When you bring up *Magical★Explorer's* Karakuri Trick Castle, the first thing that comes to the minds of the players are its secret passageways. Out of all the dungeons I had gone through, this was the one with the most secret corridors, teeming with a variety of items and skills to find, plus bosses to fight.

Despite its innumerable hidden passageways, it's possible to clear the entire place without going through a single secret path.

That said, there are just so many of the things that even a first-time player is bound to stumble across at least one of them.

I thought it was a fun design that you didn't get to see very often, so it was one of my favorite dungeons, but there was a single thing that bugged me about it. The game gives you zero hints about where a few of the secret corridors are located. To add insult to injury, those are the passageways that lead to important items, along with the goddess statue, which teaches you new skills.

Just how much blood, sweat, and tears had I shed in the hunt for this hidden path?

It was thanks to all that hard work, though, that I could take it easy right now. I had a perfect grasp of where every last secret corridor was located.

Now the question was, where were we supposed to go next once we cleared this hidden path? Going all the way back to the entrance for a moment and reentering from there was the most surefire method, so perhaps we would get the skill located relatively close to the entrance next.

As I was planning out the route in my head, Nanami spoke to me.

"You don't seem to have much to do."

"Well, I'm not exactly busy…"

I wouldn't be able to mull everything over like this if I was.

It had to be said, though, that we were currently taking a break in a safe zone, so the truth was that *we all* didn't have much to do.

"How about we pretend we're newlyweds?" Nanami asked.

"...Where'd that come from?"

Sure, we had time to kill, but I had no clue where her urge to play house had come from.

"Welcome home, Master. What would you prefer to have first? Your angel? Your maid? Or perhaps, your Na...na...mi?"

Why was she spinning around and striking a pose for each option while slowly lifting up her maid uniform? Not that it wasn't unbelievably cute, of course.

"So we're doing this whether I want to or not, huh... Heck, all those options are the same anyway. All right, then, I'll start with dinner, I guess."

"Omigooooosh ♪! You're going to eat me up?!"

"...Okay, how about a bath first?"

"Omigooooosh ♪! A bath with Nanami?! I'll wash your back!"

"So I end up with you no matter what?!"

When I quipped back, Nanami gave me a big smile. Hmm, well, if I've got to choose, I'll definitely go with the bath, thank you very much.

"Umm, so are you always doing this sort of thing, or...?"

Yuika seemed exasperated by our idiotic nonsense.

"It gets even worse sometimes, you know," Ludie flatly replied. As much as I'd love to deny it, she had me there.

"...The Hanamura house is really something, isn't it?"

"Hey, what's that supposed to mean...? Okay I can't really deny that the house has its fair share of strange people in it."

"Sure, there's a lot of *unique* types living there, but they're all good people."

Yukine had forced a smile as she replied, but I didn't think it helped much.

"Here, Master, a sandwich for you. I made sure to add *a little something* to it to ensure your lifelong love for Nanami."

"We're still going with this, are we? There's no poison or anything in here, right?"

What the hell was "lifelong" supposed to mean? That was a real worrying turn of phrase. I wasn't going to die or anything, was I?

I took a look at the sandwich she handed me. I got the feeling there were just a few more vegetables in this one compared with the one I had just finished. I figured I'd scarf it down since she'd been kind enough to make it for me.

Nanami waited for the exact moment of my first bite before chiming in.

"Oh, incidentally, Miss Ludie actually made that sandwich."

Then it all clicked.

Nanami had been biding her time for an opportunity to give me the sandwich. *Miss Ludie made this just for you, so you need to thank her* was probably what she was getting at.

Still, I felt like the strange multiple-choice question at the start was unnecessary.

"Oh, um…I know it's a bit messy compared with Nanami's, but I had some spare time, so I thought I'd try making one, is all."

"No need to worry, it's really good. Thanks."

It looked perfectly normal, and it tasted great. Ludie needed to be a bit more confident in her abilities.

"Oh, really?"

She turned away, attempting to obscure the look of delight on her face.

Now that I thought about it, everyone had been making all these small gestures toward me lately. I would need to thank them for it later.

Anyways, this sure was a tasty sandwich. Wait a sec. Tasty? Sandwich? I felt like I had just eaten one recently… But when was it, though? Hmmm. And I think it smelled sort of like a cheap energy drink? Wait, was that one from Sis? *Ngh*, my head…

"Is something wrong, Takioto?"

"O-oh, no. It's nothing. Let's rest a little bit longer before we head a bit farther in and grab the skill there," I said, which once again prompted Yuika to give me a suspicious, reproachful look.

"Ohhh, so there's a skill we'll learn up ahead, is there…?"

As I replied with a wincing smile, a thought came to me—Yuika was commenting on it candidly because she was just like that, and Yukine and Ludie had picked up on the situation themselves but were avoiding the subject on purpose.

And then another thought—I would eventually have to reveal every-thing not just to Nanami, but to Ludie and the others as well.

With our break over, we quickly started moving again.

"What sort of skill are you after?"

I hesitated slightly on whether I should answer Yuika's question in detail or not, but oh well, it was probably fine.

"The Tonsou skill."

"What's that supposed to be?"

Ninja skills were meant to be secret, so Ludie and the others prob-ably weren't aware of them. Even in the game, the player won't learn how to obtain any of them if they don't buddy up to one of the two ninja characters. It's a different story once either of them joins your party, though—they start blabbing about the skills every chance they get. Are you sure you should be doing that, ninja…?

"It's basically a skill that helps you run away from enemies."

Tonsou is a super-efficient ability that you always want to pick up when speedrunning. Fleeing encounters is vital for improving your times.

A common tactic in speedrunning role-playing games is attempting to reach the farthest town you can at low levels. That means you'll be fleeing from every single encounter on your way to somewhere you would normally get to in the latter half of the game.

But what's the point of that?

There are a number of reasons why. To get weapons that are power-ful for the early parts of the game; to befriend characters in that town and add them to your party; to gain magic, skills, and valuable items that would otherwise be a long ways off; to grab items from the houses there to power yourself up…

This is all in the interest of rapidly training your low-level characters.

Then after buying equipment from a town located in a high-level area to supercharge your offense, you level by fighting enemies you could now one-shot. This is the best possible method, efficiency-wise.

Of course, it's possible to do something similar in *Magical★Explorer*, as well—run away from all the fights in the Beginner's Dungeon and similar areas, defeat the boss with fire sigil stones, and use a similar method to clear dungeons that would be unlocked afterward. Then you could farm experience in the most efficient areas possible once you get the proper weapons and equipment together.

In truth, I had planned on doing that at first myself, and I'd already tried adopting a portion of the overall strategy.

But the thing was, this world wasn't a game.

Even if I gathered magic particles to raise my base stats, I could still lose against people like Yukine or Claris, who had a keen sense for combat.

To improve my combat abilities, I would need to spar with and confront a variety of monsters, and powerful ones at that.

Still, using a strong weapon to annihilate monsters for experience wasn't a total waste of effort.

Efficiently farming experience while also squaring off against seasoned combatants to hone your own abilities—that was the best way to go about it.

Next up, I would need to think about efficient methods of farming. Dungeons generally provided good opportunities for amassing magic particles. To accomplish this without wasting too much time, I would need to guarantee that I could flee from weaker monsters.

This is the biggest advantage of Tonsou from a speedrunning perspective, but the skill has one other effect: It raises your speed. In-game, increased speed means you act earlier in battle.

But what would high agility do in real life?

The way I was thinking, making my movement faster would be an incredible way of powering up.

With all that in mind, there was no doubt that Tonsou was an extremely useful skill to have.

We continued on our path, defeating monsters as we went, eventually coming upon what looked like a large hall. There were a number of wooden pedestals and scrolls lying around, but I honestly didn't need to look at any of them.

To obtain the Tonsou skill, you needed to do two things. First, you had to find a hidden door without any hints. Second, you had to solve a puzzle.

On the floor right before the end goal, there was a scroll with a hint that you would then use to solve said puzzle...but thanks to my knowledge of the game, I already had the answer memorized.

*   *   *

Having now obtained the Tonsou skill, which improved our ability to escape, we obviously reentered Karakuri Trick Castle and used this newfound art to flee from enemies at every opportunity...except things didn't quite go like that.

Even on our second run through Karakuri Trick Castle, we didn't ignore any of the fights with the weaker monsters, defeating them without exception as we continued on. We made sure to collect the loot they dropped, too, of course.

"There really are quite a lot of traps, aren't there?" Ludie grumbled as she jumped over the trap Nanami had identified.

"That's just the sorta dungeon it is."

If there's one thing in this dungeon I'm disappointed about, it's that the traps don't unlock character CG scenes. But even if that were the case, I would have planned on avoiding every last one with not just heartrending but full-bodied sorrow. Still, a teensy, tiny bit can't hurt, right...?

"This really is one incredible party we've got...," Yuika said keenly.

Immediately sending my fantasies to the winds and feigning composure, I asked her what she was getting at.

"What about it?"

"Even back at Susano Martial Arts Academy, you rarely ever saw teams that were this incredible."

"Seriously?"

"Oh yeah, it would totally put the upperclassmen there to shame."

"Yuika."

I turned to face who'd chimed in and found Yukine, smiling as she followed us.

"Don't worry, Takioto's group is abnormal even at Tsukuyomi Magic Academy."

"Isn't it odd to say 'don't worry' and 'abnormal' in the same breath...? Anyway, did you just lump me in with Takioto?"

I unequivocally wanted to agree.

"Speaking of Tsukuyomi Magic Academy, it's pretty wild in more ways than one."

"Wild?"

"Sure. I mean, the campus is bigger than any other school's, you move around through spatial magic circles, and there's the whole Tsukuyomi Point system, too."

"Wait, is the Academy really that out there?"

Yuika let out an exasperated and appalled gasp, glaring at me with reproach.

"Ugh, the ultrarich just don't get it, do they...? I'll take one Rosenkreuz, Inc.... No, in fact, I'll take one Hanamura Group–made magic item, please and thank you."

The Hanamura family did seem pretty eccentric.

I'd assumed they were like any other wealthy family at first, but lately, I'd been thinking about just how out there they were. The way they were treated by students of nobility was particularly striking.

"It's true. Tsukuyomi Magic Academy's facilities aren't just some of the best in the world—they're *the* best in the world," Yukine said in agreement. "I participated in a tournament with Amaterasu Academy and Susano Martial Arts Academy once, and Tsukuyomi Magic Academy unquestionably had the better facilities. Maybe that's because its students are a bit better overall."

Yuika nodded at her comments.

"Riiight, that's definitely true. But there's still plenty of really incredible students in Susano's upper ranks, too."

"You're right about that. Even I know a few examples. They may not be able to go toe to toe with President Monica, but there's one who could match up against Captain Stef. Though, I wouldn't say they're all necessarily worthy of respect..."

Who exactly was Yukine speaking so evasively about? If they were someone strong, a few candidates came to mind, but...could she have been talking about *him*?

Regardless, Yukine would soar way past all of them and stand shoulder to shoulder with President Monica.

Now then, do you think that our party, which was easily capable of clearing up to the fortieth layer of the Tsukuyomi Dungeon, would struggle against a boss in a dungeon only slightly more difficult than the Beginner's Dungeon?

Of course we wouldn't.

"*Haah...*"

Yuika sighed as she watched the secret boss guarding the treasure, Red Ogre, dissolve into magic particles.

"What's the sigh about, Yuika?"

"Now I reeeally get that I was an ignorant little frog in a tiny well."

"What do you mean?"

"You're all way too strong. No fair," she grumbled, dispersing the mana filling her hands.

Should I have let her finish off the Red Ogre?

Nanami had cut off its escape with her arrows, Ludie had hit it directly with Storm Hammer, and while it was getting pounded, I'd closed the distance to unleash my sword from its sheath and finish it with a single slash.

The boss had gone down before it could do a thing.

"Argh, looks like I'm the biggest burden here."

"You think so? Didn't seem that way at all to me. You can heal, too."

The fight had simply ended before Yuika could lend a hand, but she had been really active in defeating low-level monsters throughout the dungeon. Plus, it was a treat for the eyes just having her around. Made me want my own little sister, too.

"Spare the flattery. Do you even need any healing? I'm pretty sure it hasn't come up at all."

"Miss Yuika, Master is saying...*Don't get the wrong idea; it's not like I'm only able to charge in recklessly because I have you backing me up or anything.*"

"Why did you make me sound like a stubborn anime girl? You're *actually* gonna give people the wrong idea if you put it like that."

Also, was it just me, or had Nanami been on some weird inner-monologue kick lately?

I would have preferred Ludie or Yuika hitting me with a line like that, if anything.

Actually, if I did hear someone in real life talk to me like that, I'd probably just get annoyed, so never mind!

"Then what is it, hmm? Are you saying you're only after me for my healing?"

"Don't phrase it to sound like I'm only after your body, c'mon... Obviously that's not the case here."

"What an awful thing to say, Takioto. Nothing but a three-night, three-day suite room and a vacation in the Tréfle Empire will heal my wounded heart!" Yuika said.

"You're real shameless about what you want, huh."

I thought it was great that Yuika just spoke her mind. It made things easy to understand. Incidentally, if she asked Ludie about that vacay, she'd probably give the okay without a second thought. In one of *MX*'s updates, they patched in an event where you visit the empire's resort town, and I wouldn't mind going if given the chance.

"Nanami was right—you've got quite the quip game, Takioto."

"Wait, is this all her fault?!"

Hey, Nanami? Why're you looking so smug and making peace signs?

"Argh, whatever, it was all a joke, okay? Just a joke! But I'm really glad I came with you today. I learned a lot… Thank you. That extends to Ludivine, Mizumori, and Nanami, too. Thank you for letting me join your dungeon clear."

"Just *Ludie* is fine. Also, if you want to come to the Tréfle Empire, I can invite you, you know. The offer stands for you as well, Yukine."

"Wh-whaat?! I was just joking!" Yuika cried.

"I'll have to take you up on the offer during our next break."

Yuika was seriously freaking out, while Yukine was treating the offer like nothing. It appeared Yuika was still a bit reserved around Ludie.

"It's no big deal; Father's already been saying I'm free to bring people with me if I want. Oh, Kousuke? He wants to thank you in person, so you come, too."

So the trip was all but a done deal, then. I did want to go, but if it meant I would have to run into *that guy*, well…who knew what would happen?

As we talked, the monster had finished turning into magic stones, and Yukine came up to us after collecting the item drops.

"All right, everyone. About time we moved on."

The dungeon that was going to serve as the stage for our competition with Gabby, Twilight Path, didn't actually have to be cleared at all.

In *MX*, the player doesn't reach it until about midgame. It's one of the dungeons that unlocks when you enter the Three Committees, and it's also used for a Ceremonial Committee event.

On top of that, the Twilight Path doesn't really pose much of a challenge. Outside of the creatures lurking in its deepest sections, the enemies aren't particularly strong, either. Though, perhaps the dungeon only seems easy, since your party is pretty well equipped by the time you join the Three Committees.

If there's one thing you needed to look out for in this dungeon, it was the traps. Still, most of them could be identified with a low-level Find Traps skill, and they wouldn't prove any trouble at all thanks to the ring I'd picked up.

Furthermore, the items you could get here were proportionate to the dungeon's level, and while they were indeed valuable, they didn't appeal to me all that much. I had already gotten them in a different dungeon, and the rarity and abilities of the rings Ludie and the others were already wearing outdid the Twilight Path items anyway.

However, the dungeons added into the game as bonus content often contain good items that are disproportional to its difficulty. Those rings from before were no exception. That was the whole reason I had prioritized clearing the bonus-content dungeons in the first place.

Also, the monsters that showed up here could all be found in other dungeons, and none of them were worth mentioning. Similarly, the item drops in this place could be summed up with a resounding "meh."

In short, I didn't care about the Twilight Path, and it wasn't really worth visiting. From a pure-efficiency perspective, I would have liked to go back to Karakuri Trick Castle, which Yukine and the others were still running even now.

Despite my list of complaints, you couldn't afford to miss this dungeon if you joined the Ceremonial Committee. Especially if it was character CGs you were after. But I digress.

"You think Minister Benito's going to be much longer?"

"He's still not scheduled to be here for five minutes," Nanami replied.

"I mean, I get that he had to submit a request to use this dungeon and all, but…I'd really like to do something about this whole situation," I said, shifting my gaze to the two people quarreling in front of me.

"*Oh-ho-ho-ho!* I hope you're prepared to grovel on your knees."

"Shouldn't you be saying that about yourself?"

If memory served, Gabby had picked a fight with me first. So why did I feel a bit left out as I watched two girls, who were wearing strained smiles and glaring at each other hard enough to hear sparks flying between their eyes? No, forget being left out—I was getting left behind.

"Master, shouldn't you use a suave, debonair *voice* to mediate the situation?"

"I don't really feel the necessity in specifically using a debonair *voice*, but it might be a good idea to try to mediate things here, huh."

The two of them were using enhance magic on themselves, too. They weren't going to come to blows the next moment, right? Also, I had no idea why Nanami was emphasizing the word *voice*. That didn't stop me from imitating her in kind, though.

"Fear not, Master. I thought this might happen, so I concocted the perfect line to keep the peace. Racking my brain all night has left me quite sleep-deprived."

"Go right ahead and sleep then, instead of coming up with all this nonsense. But I guess I'll hear you out since you thought so long and hard about it."

"*Oh, my charming mademoiselles, please don't fight over me! Alas, what a cruel and wicked man I am…!*"

"That'll get Yuika to turn on me, too."

Gabby would get even more upset about it. Though on second thought, I could see Minister Benito pulling it off. It fit his aristocratic appearance, at least. Not that he'd ever say something like that.

"Don't worry. I will instantly come dashing in, cling to your arm, and—"

Nanami threw her arms around me. Nice and soft, yup, yup.

"—continue the conversation by shouting, *So was our love just a game to you?!*"

"The two of them would be too appalled to say anything. What the hell kinda soap opera are you going for here?" I asked.

What was she hoping to accomplish by making the situation even more chaotic?

Also, Nanami, don't you know that you can keep hanging on my arm a little while longer?

"After that, we'll get stranded on a deserted island with the people we met in our cooking class. Once we get wrapped up in World War Six, I'm planning for the story to have every one of us go out to subdue the Dark Demon Lord, but just imagining it is making me all choked up. We'll definitely get a movie deal out of this…!"

"Not with a plot like that…"

"The title will be nice and simple—*Holy Angel Nanami: Case File of a Maid for Hire.*"

"Okay, seriously, what the hell is up with this narrative…? And that means the woman who suddenly starts tugging on my arm is the main character! That's not going to sell, so let's call it here."

She definitely wasn't listening to me, right? Not like she ever did anyway.

"I understand your apprehension, Master. You're worried about the main theme song."

"Pretty sure the plot and themes are way more of a problem than any of the music."

I wasn't worried about the theme song to begin with. In fact, the thought hadn't even crossed my mind.

"Let's have Miss Ludie sing it for us. That will get the public interested for sure."

I couldn't argue with the fact that the Tréfle princess lending her singing voice to such an absurd and illogical movie would get people talking. Not that she would agree to begin with.

"Miss Yukine can play bass. You can leave the guitar part up to me; I've never played one before in my life."

"How can I do that when you're a total newbie?!"

And Nanami didn't have the time to start learning. In fact, did I know anyone who could play an instrument? Maybe Ludie—I could see her busting out a violin.

"Miss Hatsumi can be on the keyboard, while Master can play…the tambourine?"

"Why am I the only one you're unsure of here, huh? And why on earth would you pick the tambourine? The next instrument to come up should be drums, right? At this rate, it'll look like I'm doing karaoke instead of playing in a band!"

"For the band name, we can take everyone into account and go with *Hatsuyuki Nanalu Tambourine*."

"So I'm basically not in the name at all. Sounds like the tambourine thing is set in stone, too, then?"

The way this was panning out, the bit was going to end with me telling her to stop referring to the tambourine as *Kousuke Takioto*, wasn't it?

"You are quite the amusing fellow, Kou," Shion muttered calmly, watching us as if we were simply hilarious.

"Why am I the one who's amusing here?"

I hadn't done anything; that sentiment should've applied to Nanami, or Yuika and Gabby, who were *still* bickering with each other.

"Come now, you don't recognize it yourself…? In any event, have you heard?"

"About what?"

Shion curved her lips into a smile, poking her fan into my side as she spoke.

"Yukine invited Yuika to join the Morals Committee."

Thinking that this conversation was going to get long, Shion and I left Nanami to look after Yuika and Gabby.

I knew all about this, of course. Or rather, I had figured that this would happen. Yukine had previously shown interest in Yuika, who had a good relationship with Ludie as well. While Yuika could come on a bit strong and was sometimes grating, she was still considerate of others' feelings. I always had loads of fun talking with her.

Yuika's modesty regarding her own abilities was likely another point in her favor to Yukine. That Yuika felt the need to work hard and had actively asked to be included in our training was yet another.

If anything, it would be harder to find someone who *wasn't* interested in a person like Yuika. She was pretty, to boot.

"Yukine brought it up while I was around in the first place. To be honest, I was pretty surprised that Yuika didn't immediately give her an answer. Along with the fact that she had already been approached by the Student Council."

"Indeed. As it happens, the president came by the Ceremonial Committee some time back, and Yuika's name came up when we were discussing you."

"…Shouldn't you be keeping that information secret?"

"Oh, please, we could kick things off right now, and you'd win easily, no? I thought it better to induce a little bit of unrest to make it more interesting."

"How can you be so sure when you've never even tested me before?"

"I have seen your abilities at work. That and your solo trip to the fortieth layer in a week has me convinced. Even I couldn't accomplish that," she quietly murmured. Before I could say anything in response, Shion changed the subject.

"In regard to little Yuika, the truth is, the principal seems to have already had her eyes on her. That must have spurred the Student Council's interest, wouldn't you say?"

"I get it, so it's all because of Marino, then."

"Oh, please, it isn't only the Student Council that's shown interest, you know. The same goes for the Morals Committee. In fact, the minister and I thought it prudent to reach out to her ourselves, too. That is why I wanted to hear your opinion on the matter, you see."

"Hmm?" I couldn't help cocking my head. "Hold on a minute. The Ceremonial Committee already made a promise with Gabb—er, with Gabriella, right?"

At this, Shion put up both her hands to try to calm me down.

"Don't give me that scary look. This is all in the case that Gabriella loses here."

"Well, you're already aware of Yuika's abilities, so it seems fine to me." However…

"Gabriella can put up plenty of fight herself, though. She is clearly better than me academically, at the very least. Those grades aren't something she could've earned overnight, either."

I couldn't deny that her talents in combat were a step behind the main heroines. But Gabby had the personality to put in the effort to train if she wanted. Besides, she isn't necessarily a bad character in the game, just on par with the other sub-heroines. Some people even insisted on using her because they liked her so much. She had certainly helped me out quite a bit!

"Still...why Yuika, exactly? I don't think she really fulfills the requirements for the Ceremonial Committee myself."

The role of the Ceremonial Committee was to antagonize the student body in order to motivate them. Since the group served as the students' enemies, there were various risks that came with joining the organization.

Shion and Minister Benito were nobility. Minister Benito's young sister, Gabriella, was nobility. I myself was part of the Hanamura family. We all had a shield of power and authority to fall back on if something went wrong.

But Yuika was in a different position.

In truth, this had also puzzled me while playing the game.

I could sort of accept how *Magical★Explorer* protagonist Iori Hijiri could end up joining. To enter the Ceremonial Committee in-game, you need to satisfy one of two conditions: possessing abilities that exceed a certain benchmark, or challenging Tsukuyomi Dungeon early. In doing something like my solo forty-layer clear, you prove your capabilities and silence anyone who objects to your appointment.

What about Yuika, though?

The Student Council and the Morals Committee evaluated candidates solely on grades and actual ability, so I could understand their interest in her. But that wasn't the case with the Ceremonial Committee. If she joined as the little sister of Iori Hijiri, who possessed awe-inspiring power, then I could understand; his presence would be like a shield. However, there were some times when that wasn't the case. There was always the chance it was an event-flag bug from the devs, though.

Besides, her status as a blood descendant of the Founding Saint should've still been a mystery. So in that case?

"You, Yuika, and Nanami have been going around together lately, yes? Did you know Yuika is starting to develop a bad reputation in the student body?" Shion asked.

"Whoa, really?"

"...So you didn't, then. Well, you know now. On top of that, people are also saying that she has the protection of the Hanamura family."

"Oh, I think it's totally fine to talk about that. In fact, I'm probably the one telling people."

"With that in mind, there is the rumor that you two are friends, yes? Imagine you were a regular student—what would you think of all that?"

I'd obviously think she was trying to ingratiate herself with the Hanamuras, or that she was Kousuke Takioto's personal favorite, or... Now it clicked. I understood what Shion was getting at, sure, but I couldn't help but wince a little.

"That's what I mean."

"I get it. She's got skills, and the students think she has someone backing her up because of her relationship with the Hanamuras. Actually, I've been thinking about being there to support her after all that's happened, so it really *is* the truth."

"Fortunately, the other two committees were able to spread rumors about her being forced to talk to you. Now everyone will direct their ire at you. When it's all said and done, the girl is compatible with any one of the Three Committees."

Things were making sense now.

"I think it'd be fine to bring Yuika into the Ceremonial Committee."

It would make it a lot easier to come to her aid whenever someone after her blood tried to swoop in.

"Can I ask you one more thing?"

"What?"

"Is Minister Benito not in favor of Gabriella joining the Ceremonial Committee?"

"Hmph, yes, a difficult question... I don't have a clue."

I felt my body crumple from the shattered tension.

"Y-you don't know?"

"As if I have any idea what that man is thinking. He does appear to want her to grow, that much I will say."

That was somewhat of an explanation. There was a lot I could say here, but concisely put, Benito was definitely just as much of a doting brother in this world as he is in-game.

"But he doesn't want her to chase after him."

"Oh really..."

"Personally, I find the minister respectable. A worthy person to model oneself after."

"Perhaps something else is going on within the Evangelista family… Though, actually, is it all right for me to even say that?"

"Come now, you haven't been sworn to silence. Go ahead, you can simply say I decided it was fine to talk about, no?"

Her reasoning was a little bit twisted, wasn't it? How very Shion.

"But if I do that, it'll lead toward the bad ending, won't it?"

"Hmm, what is this 'bad ending' of which you speak?"

"Don't worry about it. It's just that I don't think Gabriella's going to join the Ceremonial Committee."

"…Because you're going to beat her?"

"Well, that's obvious, but no. It's because she has a good head on her shoulders and can stand on her own."

She had her airheaded moments, but she was a diligent girl who really thought things through.

After several more minutes, Minister Benito made his entrance.

"Looks like he's here. I suppose it is time for me to attend to my post," Shion said.

"…Things are already heating up, aren't they ♪?"

The source of this conundrum—Benito—looked over toward us with a smile, unfazed by it all.

Gabby and Yuika had both quieted down, likely because of all the abuse they had hurled around. However, I could still imagine the raging demons glaring at each other behind their backs.

There was a mountain of things I wanted to say to Minister Benito, but I figured I'd wait until later. I'd apologize to him then, too.

After all, I was going to worry him by having Gabby head to a hidden layer.

"Now, regarding the rules…are we clear?"

Despite what he said, there were hardly any stipulations. The three of us would enter the dungeon simultaneously. The one who reached Shion first, who was already on the fifth layer, would be the winner. We were free to use any weapons and items we saw fit on our way down. If we found ourselves in danger, we'd use an item to escape.

It was extremely simple.

As for why the fifth layer in particular, it was so we would come together on the layer with a floor boss.

The Twilight Path had several different routes to its deepest layers.

The simplest way of putting it was that there were four spatial magic circles to get to the next layer. Not only did each of these four circles teleport you to different a location, but since they also led to their own, independent layer, the odds that we would encounter one another were slim. Though depending on which circle we chose, there was a chance that we could end up on the same floor together.

The floors with boss battles were the one exception to this system; they only had a single version, so we would be able to meet up there.

I assumed that Shion would be waiting for us in the safe zone right before the boss.

"The rules are crystal clear. Yuika, Gabriella, and I will each take different spatial magic circles and make our way through the dungeon. The first person to reach Shion on the fifth layer is the victor. Right?"

We would all be able to easily reach the fifth already. Both me and the two girls.

Though Yuika and Gabby would definitely have an easier time exploiting enemy weaknesses in this dungeon than I would.

"Yup, looks like we're all good... Well then, we've spent plenty of time already, so let's get started. Shion should be near the goal by now. Let's head to the dungeon entrance," Minister Benito said before walking off and entering a magic circle.

"I'm overcome with laughter simply imagining you groveling on your knees! *Oh-ho-ho-ho-ho!*" Gabby declared.

"Too bad you're going to be the one groveling at the end of this," Yuika snapped.

We followed Benito and teleported to the Twilight Path dungeon.

I touched the wall and confirmed I was feeling what I was feeling, then waited for Yuika and Gabriella. Nanami appeared to have something she wanted to check for herself, so she went up to Minister Benito and started talking with him as she examined the various magic circles.

Once I made sure Yuika and Gabby had been teleported here, I walked behind them as I looked over at Nanami.

Here was where she and I planned on making a bit of a scene.

The Twilight Path also contained a few hidden floors. I planned on opening the one that would be the most mentally taxing.

As to how I would do that...I had actually consulted Nanami on the matter already.

First, she would pretend to accidentally press a switch, and while I pretended to regain my balance, I would insert a key. Yup, the plan was foolproof. We had actually rehearsed it in secret beforehand and confirmed it would be safe. Well, some monsters would show up, so it wasn't *completely* safe, but...

"Okay, so we choose one of these magic circles and head on in..."

All right, it was right about time. Nanami would hit the switch...

"Hmph, none of the paths will prove difficult for me anyway, so I'll choose the farthest right circle for *my* route!"

Gabby grinned as she spoke. Just then, she stumbled on an indent in the floor and reached her hand out to the wall to keep her balance.

Ker-chak.

Uhhh?

"Oh my!"

"Tch, if only you had fallen flat on your face..."

"How dare you sa...?"

Incensed, Gabby had started to berate Yuika, but she couldn't finish her sentence.

The ground shook with a loud rumble, as if something heavy was being dragged across the floor. I assumed that everyone besides Nanami and myself was totally confused right now, wondering what exactly had happened.

The instant after the ground stopped rumbling, a magic circle–like pattern appeared at Gabby's and Yuika's feet, and several different characters emerged on its surface.

I didn't really understand what had happened, but all's well that ends well. Now I just needed to walk up, ask everyone if they were okay, and slip the key in!

"*Eek!*"

Gabby lost her balance from another tremor, landing so perfectly on the characters on the magic circle, it was like she had been aiming for it. Then Yuika came up next to her, stepping on a few characters beneath her feet.

I just need to slip in the key...slip the...key... Huh?

The two of them had stepped on five of the letters. As the fanfare signaling the correct combination echoed, I couldn't help but mumble, "You've gotta be kidding me."

I didn't have time to stand there in shock, though. The magic circle at Gabby's feet had already activated, and particles were floating up into the air, glowing like fireflies.

Yup, there was no doubt about it—that was the magic circle to the secret layer. Except that wasn't the one I was trying to activate, was it?

Unfortunately, Yuika was close enough to Gabby to get caught in the teleportation, too. She looked over at me in blank surprise as the lights enveloped her.

See, I was supposed to be the one causing all this to happen…

…but somewhere in my mind, I had expected things to play out like this.

"Gabriella!"

Minister Benito's shout echoed through the cave right as I dived into the light. As I listened to his cry, a thought suddenly came to me.

It's not often that you get to see a look of genuine shock on Benito's face.

My vision was enveloped further and further in light.

Right before I was warped away, I noticed Nanami bowing to me, as though she was wishing me a safe trip.

It's up to you to explain everything to Minister Benito and Shion, okay?

Gabriella Evangelista was, in certain respects, a character who always lived up to expectations.

Just as her appearance suggested, she guffawed with a loud "*Oh-ho-ho-ho,*" possessed a haughty personality to match, and would occasionally betray this image with an airheaded clumsiness that actually came as little surprise. She met these expectations in battle as well.

And in a certain sense, this latest conundrum was perfectly in line with her character, too.

No normal person could stumble their way into pressing that switch on the wall, much less blindly activate and press the correct combination on the magic circle–cipher that the switch generated.

The fact that Gabby, and Ms. IOU as well, made you believe that they were totally capable of such nonsense was a really amazing and, um, charming (?) element of their characters.

If their clumsiness manifested during a truly important dungeon visit, some people might punch themselves or send a fist through their monitor, but I wasn't bothered at all.

Now, where we ended up on the other side of the teleporter wasn't an issue. It was a hidden layer of the dungeon.

While the events to get here may have been unexpected, as long as things worked out in the end, then there would be nothing... Scratch that, there may have been something to worry about. I was fairly confident I remembered *that* being at the end of this route.

If I were to point out one other thing that I hadn't planned for, it was that the magic circle spat us out in midair.

"*Eeeeeaauuuuugh!*"

"*Gaaaaaaaaaugh!*"

Suddenly engulfed in weightlessness, my surprise only lasted an instant before I immediately searched for the other two. I wasted no time heading over to them and reaching out my stole.

Yuika grabbed onto the fabric herself as she plummeted, while Gabby needed to be wrapped up and pulled toward me.

I quickly brought them close into my arms, using my muscles as a parachute... Okay, I actually stretched my stole out wide instead.

Our descent slowed slightly, but this wouldn't be enough to dampen our impact.

Convincing myself I had to protect the other two, I used enhance magic on myself. Beside me, Yuika cast defense-strengthening support magic.

Honestly, I was impressed. She had been screaming just a moment ago, but she was still capable of thinking straight in a tense situation like this. By contrast, Gabby was clinging onto me and screeching, her pure-white panties on full display. But that's what made her so cute, wasn't it?

Why had Yuika only used her support magic on me?

Well, I supposed that I technically understood the reason. It was *that* sort of thing, wasn't it? She was basically telling me, *You better do something about this, Takioto.*

I immediately stretched out my stole as wide as it would go, forming it into a parachute-like shape to slow our descent even further. I thought this would allow me to endure the impact of the landing, but it seemed my fears were unnecessary. The instant I reached the ground, the area at my feet limply caved in, and I didn't feel pain in the slightest.

It looked like the area at our feet was a cushion.

If I had to describe the feeling, it was like a water mattress. Rising from the area where I had landed, across which a slime-like cushion was stretched, I grabbed the two girls in my stole. Escaping from my strange footing, I moved to the next floor.

I took a closer look at Gabby and saw that her face was deathly pale. It was understandable. She'd been ready and raring to take on a dungeon, only for her own miraculous blunder to send us tumbling into a mysterious hidden layer. Plus, you would normally expect to die falling from that high up.

If I were to be perfectly honest with myself, I wanted to immediately bring her close and whisper in her ear that it was going to be okay, but of course, there was no way I could do that. Depending on the circumstances, that would've led me straight into a thrashing from Yuika.

Gabby was still unsettled, so I set her down and told her to not let what happened bother her. Then I began investigating the floor we were on with Yuika.

The Twilight Path hidden layer was a cave-style dungeon built from stone, just like its in-game counterpart. The walls, the floor, and the ceiling were carved out of stone, with certain areas requiring careful footing.

As always, the layer was illuminated by some unknown light source, so we didn't need to worry about visibility.

Vacantly staring down the corridor, I thought back to Gabby freaking out in my arms.

A big reason why people had nicknamed her *Gabby* was because her scream sounded like she was saying *gaaaaaaaaa*. Of course, the name *Gabriella* was normally shortened to Gabby in the English-speaking world, so that was part of it, too.

"Hmmm. It looks like going forward's our only option here... The escape items aren't responding, either."

As I stared absentmindedly down the corridor to the next floor, Yuika finished investigating the layer we had landed on, commenting on the situation as she approached.

"It's gotta be a special layer."

Certain dungeons and special floors would nullify the effects of escape items.

"The previous floor isn't going to work, either. There's no way we can climb back up there. The only saving grace here is that this area seems to be a safe zone."

Well, even if we could climb up the hole again, it would be hopeless since a magical circle had brought us here, not a pit trap or the like. As such, there was no clear evidence that there was an exit at the top anyway.

"I am so, so very sorry…"

As Yuika and I conversed, Gabby chimed in. She looked depressed, like the vigor she'd had until a moment ago had completely vanished.

"What'd I tell you? Don't even worry about it, this stuff just happens sometimes."

Contrary to her appearance—that was probably the best way to put it—she was pretty serious and had a strong sense of responsibility. That was part of why she wasn't cut out for the Ceremonial Committee.

"Let's look on the bright side here. I mean, you probably discovered a hidden room no one has ever seen before, Gabriella. There might be some unknown treasures waiting for us."

"Th-that is true. I managed to uncover a secret, didn't I…?"

My encouragement was working a bit. Despite her comment, Gabby still looked really upset. Heck, her voice was quavering.

Yuika must have known Gabby's apology was genuine. She understood that she shouldn't torment Gabby in her current state. That's why she was wearing her usual smile and keeping her mouth shut. She was definitely still annoyed, though, and I wished she would stop pinching me every time I said something to lift Gabby's spirits.

However, I was surprised that Yuika didn't look dejected or panicked like Gabby did. Of course, keeping cool was better than the alternative, but how was she able to pull that off? I knew what was coming up ahead already, but I hadn't filled her in on anything, so it would have made plenty of sense for her to be anxious and uncertain.

"Take a good look at Yuika here; she was the one who stepped on the final key of the passcode, and she's not fazed at all."

"Excuuuse me? What are you talking about, Takioto?"

Um, well, I just said it like that on purpose to help lessen Gabby's sense of guilt. I wasn't trying to put you down. Please, I'm begging you, don't get too mad. Hell, you should pick up on what I'm doing, too!

"…Well, that *is* true, but still!"

"Y-you're absolutely right! Why, if you hadn't stepped on anything, Yuika, it never would have activated!"

Please stop pinching my back Yuika. Ow, ow, don't twist like that!

"R-right, yeah! Anyway, let's hurry up and get outta here. Nanami and the others have to be worried, too."

"Yes, yes, of cooooourse. Let's run along, then."

Yuika walked off in an angry huff, and we followed along to continue onward.

Monsters would start showing up from here on out, so we needed to be careful.

"Something about this is off, don't you think?"

"What do you mean?"

"I'm talking about the three of us teaming up to fight together," Yuika said before she got in close to the sand-throwing hag and punched her light magic–enhanced gauntlet into the monster's gut. As the sand-throwing hag's body lifted off the ground, Yuika sent out a flurry of superhuman jabs straight out of a fighting game at the creature.

But the other monsters weren't content watching the sand-throwing hag get pummeled. The imp that appeared at the same time set its sights on Yuika and cast low-level dark magic.

"Takioto."

Naturally, I was already moving before she opened her mouth. I stretched out my stole, deflecting the dark magic, and took a step forward to close in on the adorably resentful imp before I stopped; a spear of light had come flying from behind me.

"Feels off, you say? Why, that should be my line."

Light Spear, a mid-level light spell, would shoot out a different number of javelins depending on the caster's abilities. While Gabby was still only sending out one, the fact that she was able to use mid-level magic at all at this point was proof that she was a member of the elite… apparently. That was how Gabby described it, so I assumed she must be right.

The imp hit with the light spear crashed to the ground, and its body slowly changed into magic particles.

I couldn't hold back a sigh as I saw the imp get struck with its weakness… This was clearly a handicap against me, right? There was no other way of looking at it.

The sand-throwing hag, imp, and even the boss that waited further in the dungeon all happened to be monsters that were weak to light magic. Even a normal descent to the fifth layer of the Twilight Path put you up against foes that were all weak to light.

That meant Yuika and Gabriella, with their light-magic proficiency, would shine their absolute brightest here. But with Yuika's preference for melee combat and Gabby's preference for long-ranged attacks, there was at least a difference in range between them.

"Wow, Gabriella, that's incredible!"

"Yes, well, it is only to be expected."

"Oh yeah, sure is amazing, all right."

I couldn't suppress the strained smile as I listened to the mumbling next to me: "Geez, we don't even know what to expect up ahead, and she's just firing off mid-level magic like it's nothing. What is she thinking?" Personally, I was feeling relieved to see Gabby gradually regain her usual demeanor. Besides, if she ran out of mana, I could just donate some of mine.

Since it didn't look like another shouting match was on the horizon, I moved toward the sand-throwing hag, which was slowly disappearing into magic particles.

When I first saw this monster in-game, I didn't think it was a sand-throwing hag at all. Based on its name alone, you'd assume it would be a wrinkled old crone.

Well, the tattered and frayed long white hair and the deep wrinkles on her face did make her look elderly. Except not only was her mouth extra-large and lined with fangs, but she also had small horns growing out of her head. There was no denying she looked more like an *oni* than anything.

Picking up the small magic stone, I moved on forward together with the other two.

About an hour later, we came upon an enormous door and a safe room.

"Is this a boss floor, then? This was much shorter than I expected."

"Quite. Even the Beginner's Dungeon is longer."

Both Gabby and Yuika were surprised to have reached the boss room

not even an hour after our exploration of the Twilight Path had gotten underway.

"That's one of the things you see a lotta times with displacement traps."

There were several types of displacement traps.

The most common type were ones that would transport you to a different section of the same layer to try to screw with your sense of direction. Since you were simply being sent somewhere on the same floor, you could use escape items to get out of the situation.

The second most common were these kinds of traps, where they send you to a special event floor, event layer, or monster house. For event layers and monster houses, clearing said floor would send you back to your original location or let you continue down to an even deeper layer in the dungeon.

In cases where you returned to the previous layer, the place you'd end up would often be rather tight and constrained. By contrast, in the event that you advanced deeper into the dungeon, you would find yourself in a vast and sprawling area or a zone with a high encounter rate.

I assumed this was all the product of game-balance considerations.

This event layer was the type that would send you back to the original layer at the end, so it was of an appropriately constrained size.

"I wonder what's waiting for us up ahead."

"Whatever it is, I bet the three of us'll be just fine… Better keep our wits about us," I said before enchanting my stole with light. Then I pushed open the door with my Third Hand. Despite how huge it was, I hadn't needed to put much force behind it. If anything, it felt a bit like the door had opened automatically.

On the other side of the door was a wide-open space. It was about the size of an elementary school playground.

Activating my mana and slipping through the door, I heard a roar echo from above after advancing a few steps inside.

"Gwoooooooooooooooooooooar!"

It was the kind of cry that pierced right through you. It made me feel as though I had been showered with electricity from head to toe.

Just then, I saw a ball of black flame come down on us from above, so I opened my stole. Then I drew Gabby, staring blankly up at the sky, and Yuika, filling her arms with mana, into my embrace.

It was a good thing that I'd made sure to enchant my stole with light.

The attack disappeared the instant it hit my stole, sizzling like fire doused with water, and a single speck of black flame fell down in front of Gabby.

At that exact moment, the monster descended down from the sky.

"Hrk! This thing *reeks*!"

Yuika's face contorted as she brought her hand to her nose.

A putrid stench hung in the air, and then a pitch-black dog put its four limbs down on the ground in front of us, its gray eyes completely devoid of pupils or irises. This was…

"The Rotting…Hellhound, huh."

"Gwoooooooooooooooooooooar!"

It must have been emitting strange sonic waves, as it felt like a small current of electricity was crackling through the area.

The Rotting Hellhound was the secret boss of the Twilight Path. In-game, it isn't a particularly strong foe, and you should be able to take it down without issue if you've built yourself up enough to join the Three Committees. It definitely *shouldn't* have been a problem, but…

"Whew, boy, this thing looks *preeeetty* tough."

I couldn't tell if that came down to the intensity of its appearance or an effect of the Roar skill it possessed. It was probably both.

"Excuse me, Takioto. I'm glad you protected me and all, but can you let go? This is approaching sexual harassment territory."

I reluctantly unwrapped my arm from around Yuika's waist, and she immediately used enhancement magic on herself before casting support magic to raise our abilities.

When Gabby realized she had been buffed with support magic, she shuddered in surprise.

Her expression suggested she had only just now become aware of the situation we were in.

"Sorry for pulling you in out of nowhere like that. You all right?"

"Y-yes. Of course I am."

This was bad. Gabby had tears in her eyes, and she hadn't used any enhance magic on herself yet. Had she never gone up against the Roar skill before? To be fair, you probably wouldn't encounter it unless you wandered into every dungeon you came across.

"Is this your first time fighting against a monster with Roar? I was the same way in the beginning."

Anyone would be quaking with fear at hearing that. That being said...

"These sorta monsters are gonna start showing up a lot more, so you better get used to them now."

...I just needed to get her mind off the fear somehow.

"Ah...!"

But the monster wasn't going to give me the time to do so.

I sized up the Rotting Hellhound running at us and stepped forward without missing a beat. Its body was likely ten to thirteen feet long. It was bigger than I thought it would be, but I didn't find it scary.

This must have been from clearing Tsukuyomi Academy Dungeon. Either that, or the fruits of my training.

I sent my Third Hand into its foreleg, which was bigger than my face, as it attempted to maul me. The Hellhound's attack had a fair bit of heft to it. When it got closer, the stench was almost enough to break my concentration. That was the extent of it, though.

Flexing my legs to withstand the assault, I repelled its forelimb. Then as though she had been waiting for this perfect chance, Yuika punched the monster as hard as she could.

"*Gwoooan!*"

"*Bleeerk*, it's sooooo stinky! Its rancid BO is enough, but somehow, its breath's even worse?! Come fight us after you shower and brush your teeth!"

"Its whole body looks rotten, so I don't think that'll do much."

The Hellhound bounded toward us as we engaged in this truly pointless conversation.

"I'm not looking to hear any sound arguments right now!"

Yuika calmly evaded the monster. In the interest of protecting our rear, I decided to take the attack head-on.

I placed a hand on my katana, grabbed the Hellhound's leg with my Fourth Hand, and swung my sword at its stomach.

"*Nghaooooon!*"

"Okay then, what do you want me to say?"

A line formed on its stomach, and a liquid resembling diluted black ink gushed from the wound.

"You're supposed to just smile and nod to girls' opinions! Still though,

I've never felt this strong, even after sparring with Yukine. Maybe it's 'cause this thing stinks so bad?"

Nevertheless, its wound slowly began to close back up. It was activating a kind of self-recovery ability inherent to some undead and slime-type monsters.

Buying some time for its wound to heal as best it could, the Hellhound opened its maw and launched black flames at us.

"True, I agree with absolutely everything you just said."

"Yikes, randomly agreeing with everything like that is so cowardly. Unbelievable," Yuika said while she hid behind me.

"Then what the hell do you want me to do?!"

Still facing forward, I adjusted Yuika's position behind me with my left arm. Then I stretched my stole out wide and defended against the black flames flying our way.

"Y'know, Nanami had it right. It really is a lot of fun talking with you, Takioto!"

"Really? I'm glad to hear it. I'll chat with you as much as you'd like after this fight. More importantly, this thing's weak to light, so be sure to enchant yourself, okay?"

"If you insist, then go ahead and do it for me, Takioto!" she said, touching her gauntlet against my hand.

"What do you mean, 'If I insist?' Sheesh."

"Heh-heh-heh-heh ♪!"

When the flames died down, Yuika sprung forward as if she'd been waiting for this exact moment. Then she punched straight into the Hellhound with the gauntlet I had just enchanted with light.

I didn't really need to worry about Yuika at all. She could probably bring down the Hellhound on her own, just like me. The problem was with Gabby.

"Hey, you good back there?"

"O-of course, I'm just fine!"

She was finally returning to normal, but she still seemed a bit rattled.

"It's okay. You saw me just now, right? I'll block all the attacks that come your way, Gabby, so rest easy and cast light spears, support magic, and healing magic for us if anything happens. I'm not too great at long-ranged magic, see... So it's up to you, Gabby. I'm counting on you."

"J-just leave it to me, then!"

After watching Gabby activate her mana, I dashed forward. I slammed into the Hellhound with my Third and Fourth Hands while the creature was locked in a fierce battle with Yuika.

"Everything okay?" Yuika asked.

"She should be all right now. Better yet, are you okay?"

"Oh, please, Takioto, are you even watching this fight? I've got this *tooootally* under control, to-ta-lly!"

"I'm more worried about what comes after this fight, actually, since I figure that gauntlet of yours will end up smelling rank as all hell."

"*Gaaaaah!* Don't tell me that, it's not even funny!"

A weapon that smells awful, huh… That's basically a curse, right?

As we kept up our asinine conversation, we sent the Hellhound flying with a punch, which was then followed by a single spear soaring out from behind us.

"*Yeeeoooan!*"

That was the shrillest cry we had heard yet. The light spear must have done quite a number on the beast.

To my delight, it looked like I wouldn't need to use any mid-level light sigil stones since Gabby and Yuika were with me.

I would have plenty of opportunities to use them in the future, so I was happy I could save some here.

Yuika launched another attack at the flinching Hellhound. It really seemed to detest light-based attacks.

The monster released another yelp and lashed out in pain, likely in an attempt to find an escape.

But after a second light spear was driven into its body, the Hellhound started moving differently.

The previous javelin had left it wincing.

Which was why Yuika thought things would go the same this time and tried to follow up with her own attack. However, the Hellhound recklessly swiped at her again with its foreleg.

Yuika just barely evaded the attack. But it must have scraped her a little bit. A red streak had formed across her chest.

"Make sure you use Cure Poison when you heal yourself, Yuika!"

"Yuuuuck, it's so stinky… What am I going to do if it gets into my clothes?!" she said before falling back. Nevertheless, the Hellhound didn't pursue her as she retreated. Instead, it stepped sideways as it observed us. Then—

"Gwoooooooooooooooooar!!"

—it roared before spitting black flames at Yuika. Yet strangely, these didn't have the same momentum as the ones before. Then it dashed forward, not at Yuika, but at Gabby.

Gabby, who was now disarmed by its roar.

—Yuika's Perspective—

Uh-oh, I thought. But it was too late.

The Hellhound closed in on Drills Girl. I could understand why she would recoil from its roar, but she couldn't let herself be so shaken by it. Still, I had to admit that Takioto never failed to impress—he was already moving to cover her.

In fact, he had always kept close enough to protect her if necessary while he was fighting the Hellhound, so there was never any question of him reaching her in time.

"Hnraaaaaah!"

With a yell, he sent his stole-fist flying into the much bigger Hellhound.

The punch connected directly with the monster as it charged at Drills, sending it flying back toward the wall with a loud *smack.* However, it immediately got to its feet, shook its head, and glared at Takioto.

Takioto glanced over at Drills and grinned in an attempt to reassure her. He immediately returned his focus to the Hellhound, stepping directly between it and Drills.

"Sorry, pup. You're not taking a step past this point," Takioto said before he approached the Hellhound, totally collected. One step at a time, his hand on his katana, an almost impossibly huge amount of mana radiating from his body all the while.

This seemed to scare the Hellhound, and it gritted its teeth in a low growl as it slowly walked sideways.

When it got around three feet within range of Takioto, it took a large jump backward. The Hellhound, retreating, and Takioto, advancing. The spectacle spoke volumes.

This was Kousuke Takioto.

This was what he was like.

For how much of a pervert he was, he was still irritatingly strong, annoyingly badass, and frustratingly kind.

Takioto didn't need either Drills or me here to fight this beast. He could've brought it down all by himself if he felt like it, without even breaking a sweat.

The Hellhound lifted its head and opened its mouth.

"*Gwooooooooooooooooooar!!*"

A jolt went through me. Seriously, was that supposed to be intimidating?

As I watched Takioto saunter toward the Hellhound, a smile on his face, I couldn't help hearing it as a terrified cry.

Suddenly snapping back to reality, I checked to see how Drills was holding up.

I wondered what had happened as I watched her stare blankly at Takioto, a hand on her chest. Growing worried, I prepared to cast recovery magic and, from her side, asked to make sure she wasn't injured.

But in her case…

"Ahhh…I don't know if I can do anything about *this*," I said.

…she was a goner. In a way, I had been too late. Though, I sort of got the feeling it had only been a matter of time.

A slightly red tinge to her cheeks. Heavy breathing. Drills clutching her chest as she gazed ardently. Hearts were floating in her eyes.

I feel like I had let myself worry for nothing. I released the tension from my body and let out a sigh.

I could understand her feelings.

When he was in a dungeon, Takioto was an aggravatingly hot dude. I mean, I guess he was pretty good-looking normally, too. He was the type of guy you warmed up to the more you got to know him.

Though, I was sure that people who were manipulated by the false image he put out there, who judged him before they looked at him, wouldn't even think so.

But if you had the chance to interact with him like his classmates had, then you would come to see him in the proper light. And the more deeply involved with him you got, well…

"What're you doing? C'mon now, snap out of it."

When I cast healing magic on her, Drills flinched with surprise and stared at me. I wondered what she was going to say. Right as she opened her mouth to speak, there came a loud *crunch* from some kind of collision, and we both turned to look toward Takioto.

We were greeted with the Hellhound falling to the ground, one of its forelimbs missing.

Takioto quickly closed the distance before returning his katana to its sheath, only to unleash it again.

My eyes couldn't keep up with his swordsmanship. The same must have gone for Drills beside me. By the time I realized what had happened, his katana was back by his side, and the Hellhound lay perfectly still.

Still glaring at the Hellhound, Takioto backed about three feet away from it, putting space between himself and the monster. Then he slowly returned his katana to its sheath. Right as he did, the monster's head fell to the ground with a perfectly timed *thump*.

Seeing this, Takioto untensed his shoulders, dispersed his mana, and took a deep breath…

…and broke into a coughing fit.

"*Bleeeegh*, this thing *reeks*!"

What an idiot. It was glaringly obvious that would have happened if he inhaled right in front of the source of the stench.

Takioto practically fled from the rotting monster before unsheathing his sword again and hesitantly giving it a sniff.

What in the world was he doing?

……………

I also brought my gauntlet up to my face and sniffed it.

It was fine. Probably.

If not, then I'd jokingly smile and demand Takioto compensate me for it, before either getting it repaired or buying a new one. I had some misgivings about the price of both options, but I was sure it would work out.

Takioto hastily collected the dropped magic stones before walking over in our direction. However, despite defeating the boss, his face didn't show any joy.

"That thing absolutely stank."

Were those really the first words to come out of his mouth after defeating a boss? Really? Not that I didn't understand where he was coming from.

As I watched Takioto slump his shoulders, a thought came to me.

A situation like this was one in a million. Why not take the opportunity to tease him a bit?

"Hold up, I ask that you keep outside a fifteen-foot radius, thank you very much…"

I put my hand up to my nose and averted my face with a grimace.

"Oh, c'mon, you can't be serious…!"

My comment got the perfect response.

"Tee-hee, I'm not. Just kidding. Good job," I said, casting healing magic on Takioto. He didn't look to be injured at all, but better safe than sorry.

However, he put his clothes up to his face and gave another anxious sniff. It looked like I didn't have any other choice, and I grabbed his arm and brought it up against my nose and chest, making sure that Drills had a good view.

"See, look? You're totally fine."

Takioto really was a perv after all.

"Y-you don't say. Still want to hop in a bath, though. Are you okay, Gabby—Gabriella?"

Drills jumped as she stared at me intently—

"O-oh, uh, yes, o-of course I'm fine… Well."

—and replied in a faltering voice. In some ways, she was anything *but* fine.

"Also, um…earlier, I believe you, well, called me Gabby…?"

"Ahh," Takioto mumbled, his face contorting for a moment. "Well, you know how it is…," he said. Despite this, he couldn't get the next words out.

It was novel getting to see Takioto so flustered. "Gabby," huh?

There was a metallic groaning sound, and I suddenly came to my senses. I'd accidentally been squeezing down on my gauntlet.

"S-sorry, it's just sorta easier to say, so… But I'll be sure to say Gabriella from no—"

"Gabby is perfectly fine with me! In fact, I insist on Gabby!"

Takioto was taken aback by the sudden volume in Drills' voice.

"S-sure, got it. Okay, then… Gab—"

Hearing where Takioto was going, I knew it'd be bad news to let him continue.

"Well, all righty then, don't mind if I do, Gabby!"

Before I knew it, I was interrupting Drills, who looked very happy, before she could reply. Both she and Takioto were caught off guard.

"I—I wasn't talking to *you*!"

"Okay, I'll go with Drills, then."

"Ex*cuse* me, are you trying to pick a fight?!"

"Gabby it is! Looking forward to getting to know you, *Gabby*!"

Her lip was twitching in anger. But I wasn't planning on backing down. I sorta didn't want the nickname to be for only Takioto to use.

Since that made me just a bit jealous.

Everyone went quiet for a few seconds, until Takioto suddenly sighed.

"So for this little competition of ours...how are we going to decide the results?"

Now that he mentioned it, that had been what we'd come here for.

"We're all tired at this point, so why don't we do it some other day?" I said, prompting Gabby to mutter her disapproval.

"What's up, Gabby?"

"I have gotten an all too bitter taste of the strength you both have. I am forced to admit that I have been defeated in both ability and mental fortitude," she admitted, her previous vigor now gone.

Seeing this, Takioto tapped Gabby's shoulder with a friendly smile on his face.

"Hey, Gabby, mind if I ask why you're so hung up on me and the Ceremonial Committee in the first place?"

Gabby genuinely looked tortured that she had wrapped us both up in her blunder. This was the second time, which made it feel even worse. She seemed pretty discouraged.

"Why?"

"Yeah. You're lashing out at me because of something to do with the Ceremonial Committee, right? Or Minister Benito, more specifically," Takioto asked.

"You're absolutely right, yes...but before I speak any further, allow me to apologize. I am truly very sorry. Takioto. And to you as well, Yuika."

"Nah, it's fine. I was never mad at you from the start, Gabby. Though, I may have some choice words to send Minister Benito's way," Takioto said with a smile. He was so frustratingly charming in moments like these.

Ah, whatever. More importantly, I needed to apologize, too.

"I sorta feel like I went a bit too far with some of the things I said, too… Sorry, Gabby."

"Not at all. It was only natural you'd be upset," Gabby said before turning her eyes away from the two of us to stare at the dungeon wall. Then she abruptly looked at the ground and began to speak, as though she was confessing her sins.

"First, I need to clarify something… I admire and look up to Brother. That is why I wished to join the Ceremonial Committee and be just like him."

I had sort of guessed that much.

"I first grew irritated at Takioto because I thought he'd bought his grades."

Takioto listened carefully to Gabby's words, an earnest look on his face.

"I find it embarrassing to admit, but I do not possess the kind of talent that Takioto, Brother, or Miss Monica have, for example. My abilities are average. I have always worked hard to compensate for this. Both in my studies and in magic."

Gabby made it sound like nothing, but I could tell that she had put in quite a serious amount of effort. Otherwise, it would have been impossible for her to get the best grades in her year.

"I simply thought that getting to the fortieth layer was an impossible feat. Impossible without resorting to some cowardly trick, of course. I wondered how someone could be content knowing that they had cheated their way to the top. But more than that, what vexed me was the delight in Brother's voice when he spoke about Takioto. He couldn't stop theorizing about how you'd pulled off your clear. And after that, Takioto joined the Ceremonial Committee."

Hearing this, something clicked inside me.

"I was jealous. Jealous of you. When Brother approved Takioto joining the Ceremonial Committee and rejected me, my envy grew even stronger. It was then that I charged out to accost you."

Gabby bit her lip as she spoke of her regrets.

"I wanted to be just like Brother, but I wasn't able to."

Takioto let out a small sigh.

"Who is your brother to you, Gabby?"

"My brother…is a genius, an exemplar, the best person in the world, and above all else, a kind person," Gabby insisted. "Our parents have always been very busy people. Father and Mother never looked after me. They did, however, pay attention to my brother. He was very smart, you see. Athletic, as well. Very proficient in magic, too. On top of all that, he was also a beautiful child."

Then very quietly, she added, "I always played by myself," before continuing:

"Regardless of the excessive expectations Father placed on him, my brother managed to exceed them time and again. So naturally, he drew people's interest. The servants at our home, our friends, they all praised my brother up and down."

Gabby struggled to get out her next statement.

"That's why I look up to my brother."

"Because he was good at magic and good at school?"

At my question, Gabby shook her head with an ephemeral smile.

"It's not because of either of those things. No, it was because I was amazed at how much praise he received from Mother and Father."

I had no idea what to say in response.

"I must have longed to be recognized by my brother...because he was recognized by my parents."

"I get it."

Takioto nodded at Gabby's words.

"So I gave it my all, day in, day out. The maid who served me would always praise and encourage me when I did. Then I managed to earn good grades. While my parents reacted tepidly to this, my brother praised me incessantly, going on about how good a girl I was, how amazing I was."

Ahh, I figured. From there, her respect for her brother must have continued to grow, alongside her dependence on him.

"I loved when Brother would commend me. But Brother has been cold lately, and he's started singing Takioto's praises instead. I couldn't stop myself from getting incensed at this."

She must have thought of pulling Takioto away from her brother by joining the Ceremonial Committee herself at that point.

"The truth is, you see," Gabby began, "I have no delusions about myself. I know that I cannot abide any underhandedness or cowardice. I like things fair and square. I am well enough aware that I won't be able to play the villain."

Now things made sense. Minister Benito was pulling the strings behind the scenes here. Takioto knew, too, and had joined this whole charade on purpose.

"I am not a good liar."

I could tell that from talking with her. For better or worse, Gabby was straightforward and direct.

"That's why I realize I am not cut out for the Ceremonial Committee. Yet I still wished to be like Brother."

Before this, I couldn't understand why Takioto never objected to Gabby or complained about her. If anything, he supported her. But now things were clear.

He had known that Gabby was actually a very diligent worker. That was why he also knew she wouldn't be a good match for the Ceremonial Committee, where she would have to bear the student body directing their animosity toward her.

Gabby's admiration for her big brother, her natural strengths and weaknesses, and her jealousy. They all jumbled together into a mess, leading her to charge after Takioto.

"I imagine Minister Benito wanted you to be more independent," Takioto said.

"Independent?"

"He didn't want you to be so tied to him. He wants you to stand on your own two feet, to think, make decisions, and move forward yourself."

Listening to this conversation, I realized something. This very moment would be a turning point for Gabby.

"Being independent means that you can do what you want, but things get really hard. There's all sorts of stuff you don't understand, you can't see what lies up ahead, and you don't have a path laid out before you."

Takioto laughed as he said this.

"*Ha-ha.* But you know, that's still fun. And as time goes on, you'll understand that there's a whole wide world out there, teeming with so many things for you to do."

Ahhh, it was so irritating. Absolutely maddening, truly aggravating. He was just, just so damn cool, I swear.

"Gabby, you're able to look hard at yourself, and you're capable of thinking things through. That's why you can stand on your own. It'd be good for you to show that to your brother, too."

She stared vacantly at the ground.

"You need to do some introspection, Gabby, and come up with the answer. Ask yourself what it is you want to do."

A thought crossed my mind—I would probably have an easier time relaying Takioto's point to her than he would. Because I had my own brother problems, just like Gabby did.

"Takioto, a minute?" I said, calling him over. Then in a quiet voice, I said:

"Let me and Gabby talk alone."

Takioto grinned and brought his face up to my ear. Then he whispered, "I'm counting on you," before putting some space between us.

"You know I have a big brother of my own, right?"

"The one on the Student Council?"

"That's him. To be honest, he's really wishy-washy. And I'm, like, sure his body is composed of about seventy percent sugar."

"Is that so?"

"Suuuuure is. But the thing is, he's kind. And he manages to be just the teensiest bit reliable when it really matters."

Not nearly as much as Takioto, though, and it was a seriously rare occurrence.

"It sounds like you have quite the older brother."

"Well, yes, he is a good sibling. Come to think of it, I wanted to get stronger when I was a kid to avoid causing trouble for him."

In the past, I was stronger than Iori. Before coming to Tsukuyomi Magic Academy, I was definitely the more powerful sibling.

But then I'd lost.

"But he actually beat me in a sparring match recently. And you know what? I felt really irritated that it happened. He's just supposed to be my stupid big brother, and now he's gotten all strong on me. I really hate losing."

Takioto smiled dryly.

"I actually did a lot of thinking while I was challenging dungeons with Takioto and everyone. *Why's my big brother as strong as he is now?* Hey, Takioto, did my brother's urge to get stronger have anything to do with me?"

Sheesh, he can't help letting that show on his face, can he? I was taking a pretty random shot there, but I guess I really hit the mark, huh?

"Takioto also pushed him to get stronger. To give a simple

explanation here, I was kidnapped once before, and my big brother tried to protect me."

"You have a lovely brother."

"And you do, too. Well, anyway, I don't want to give my big brother any more trouble, and I don't want to lose to him, either, and Takioto here goes off about being the strongest or whatever, which is truly irritating. So that made me decide I want to get stronger, too."

"Whoa, whoa, don't turn me into a punch line. Also, you're going to have a bone-crushing time if you make Iori your goal," Takioto said.

"Aw, but you're the perfect punch line. And why is trying to top my big brother going to be so hard to achieve?"

Here I was trying to get strong enough to physically crush my brother's bones, if possible.

"I'm planning on becoming the strongest around, but there's no question that Iori's gonna be the biggest wall to climb. He'll be on President Monica's level someday, just you watch," Takioto insisted.

"Then all I need to do is get more powerful than that, right? Oh, but that would make me the strongest, wouldn't it?"

Gabby laughed as we bantered with each other. Then we caught her case of the giggles, too.

"*Tee-hee-hee*, the thought came to me as I saw you both talking. How envious I am, and how I'd like to act more like myself, too."

"Envious? Of us?"

"Yes. That's right. Why, the two of you are both living very much how you wish to live, yes?"

I had to agree that Takioto and I were living while being true to ourselves. Especially Takioto—he was a total free spirit at this point.

"I wouldn't try to take many pages from his book if I were you. You know what this weirdo does? Every morning, he gets up, casually runs a dozen or so miles, does the same exact practice swing for over half an hour, and then spars against people in the Hanamura house. This is almost *daily*, mind you."

"What, that's not normal?" he asked.

It absolutely wasn't normal for the average magic-user, but well, Yukine was just as bizarre for going along with him, and Ludie looked to be going through some intense training of her own. The truth may have simply been that everyone around him was strange, too.

"From there, he'll head into a dungeon almost every day to train himself. Every once in a while, he'll come to school for Ceremonial Committee work. He'll also do really bizarre stuff at times, like making a household budget for some random person's family or managing allowances and stuff, I don't know."

"Budgeting and managing allowances? What in heaven's name…? *Tee-hee.*"

"Hold on, that look tells me you don't believe me… He really does, though. Right?"

"There are some deeper circumstances at play there, but don't worry about it."

Takioto sounded seriously exhausted, but whatever, I wasn't particularly interested in the first place.

"Anyway, getting back to his training routine—he's doing an absurd amount of stuff. So him getting stronger is inevitable."

"I had no idea Takioto went so far… I feel a bit embarrassed for even declaring war like that in the first place."

"Now that I think about it, I've seen people complain about Takioto before, but it's ironic, really. I mean, they all say things like *He's always goofing off; he bought his enrollment with his family's wealth*, but the way I see it, he puts in several times more hard work than any of his detractors."

Oh, wait, Gabby said the same thing, too, didn't she? Takioto and I both smiled awkwardly. Setting that aside, then.

"I would have known if I had just thought things through. Simply being a prodigy still wouldn't make something like that possible. My image of you has changed, indeed," Gabby said, nodding meekly.

"The only thing is, sure, I really think he's an amazing dude, but he's also a huuuge perv, which really drops my opinion of him to the floor."

Gabby couldn't hold back a chuckle at her comment. Takioto went pale.

"Okay, I'm sorry, about eighty percent of that was a lie. He's really not that amazing."

"It's not that I'm worried about! Take back the pervert stuff, dammit!"

Gabby looked to have gotten some of her spirits back.

"I think it'd be best to stop and think things through about the Ceremonial Committee and your brother, and about yourself as well, Gabby."

"Yes…I will. There's just one thing, Yuika."

"What?"

"Thank you."

She smiled, looking as though she'd finally come to her senses.

"I…have lost here today, so I will be leaving school."

"Huh, but we weren't even competing with each other, so the competition isn't valid, right?"

"I want to make things right."

This girl was a real stickler for the rules.

I mean, she was on the verge of tears here. If she was that broken up, then she should just stay, right…? She did seem *pretty* stubborn, though.

What was the correct call here…?

"All right, then that means I've won. Hey, Gabby, do you remember our promise?"

Huh?"

"Wait a sec, Takioto, what are you talking about?! You looking to get pulverized here?"

How stupid could he be? She was seriously going to quit school if he talked like that!

Nevertheless, Takioto ignored me and continued:

"Well, you remember, right?"

"Our promise? Ah."

In addition to quitting school, she'd promised to prostrate herself and… Ohhh, there was something else. The part about doing whatever Takioto told her. This was Takioto, after all—he must have made her swear to that because he'd been anticipating a scenario like this.

I hated feeling like I was dancing in the palm of his hand…

"Kousuke Takioto! You perv! Fiend! Brute!"

…so I decided to cuss him out for the time being.

"Oh, cram it, like I was ever going to say something like that! *Ahem*, Gabby."

"…What is it, then?"

"You lost to me, so you have to do as I say."

Gabby braced herself.

"I want you to show me your smiling face at the Academy. Not the face you've worn this whole time today, but a true-blue smile. And," Takioto added with a wink, "this'll be in effect until all of us graduate, okay?"

Gabby broke out into an almost disturbingly loud sob; when she finally calmed down, we began to move on.

"Yuika?"

"What's wrong, Takioto? Why the whisper?"

"This probably won't come up for a little while, but I think I'll need you to help me out with some stuff involving the Saint and the situation with Gabby's family. It's in your hands when the time comes, okay?"

"I don't mind if I can help out, but why's the Saint coming up all of a sudden?"

"Because the Evangelistas are involved with the Saint. Don't worry about it too much, though; I'll have more details for you once I'm done investigating things."

Where was he getting this information anyway? Was he leveraging the Hanamuras' connections? It piqued my curiosity a little, but I let it drop for the time being.

"All right, let's hurry through the rest of this dungeon and get out of here. If the boss showed up, that means there should be a treasure chest and the exit up ahead!"

When I started walking off to the spatial magic circle that had appeared upon defeating the boss, Takioto shouted a loud "AHH!"

Then he approached me in a panic.

"H-hold up a minute here."

"What's wrong?"

"Oh, uh, you know. You ever suddenly get the urge to take the long way around?"

"Huh?" I couldn't hold back my confusion. "Where the heck is this coming from? It's a straight shot from here, isn't it?"

We had no choice but to continue forward.

"Y-yeah, you're right, but...I've got a really bad feeling about what's coming up ahead."

Speak for yourself. I wasn't feeling anything whatsoever.

"Is there even another path to take? C'mon, let's go! C'mon, Dril—er, Gabby! You too!"

After saying this, I pushed Takioto from behind into the magic circle ahead of us, before Gabby, looking as if she had something she wanted to say, stepped into it with me.

Waiting there for us on the other side was a single treasure chest, along with some type of magic circle and what appeared to be a pro-jector. There was also an inactive spatial magic circle.

"Why, a treasure chest!"

And one that had appeared after defeating a boss, at that. It was impossible not to have high expectations. There didn't seem to be any traps, so I asked Takioto if it was okay to open it, at which he nodded with a look of grim resignation.

Although I felt like something was clearly off with the way he was acting, I decided to just open the chest first.

Chapter 8　(A Wet and Wild Dungeon　Magical★Explorer)

Reborn as a Side Character in a Fantasy Dating Sim

"Are these...clothes...?"

Inside the chest were five articles of clothing of different colors and shapes.

I mean, what was I getting cold feet about at this point? I had been prepared for this from before we had even come here, right?

In Yuika's hands were some clothes. The type of outfit you'd see a magical girl wear. Unfortunately, they weren't the frilly variety that would show up in a Sunday-morning-anime timeslot...but rather the racy kind that featured in the anime that ran after midnight.

"I feel quite the mysterious power from these."

"Pretty safe to say they've got some sort of enchantment on them."

"While that may indeed be the case...this design is quite, um…"

"Seriously, these are super risqué! Super embarrassing. I wouldn't feel comfortable in these no matter how good their abilities are."

Whoa now, hold on, there are a few who would leap at the opportunity to put these on, okay?! On top of that, some characters get huge buffs to their stats if you force them into magical-girl cosplay, okay?! Like Vice President Fran, with her diligent and serious glasses-girl look. She complains about how it's oh so embarrassing to wear, but the truth is she really yearns to put it on. It looks fantastic on her, to boot.

Okay, okay, none of that was important right now.

What was I going to do? For the time being, I supposed we needed to fill the magic circle with mana and start up the projector. I wanted to verify that things were going to be the same as in-game.

I sent mana into the projector's magic circle. When I did, Yuika jumped a bit and looked at me, but with the image and ancient writing now clear on display, I decided to ask about what was bothering her later and stared at the images.

"And what would that be, then?" Gabby asked.

"…Good question. I can't read the writing, but the picture sort of makes it clear. Let's see, this is an image of someone wearing the clothes in the treasure chest and going on an adventure," Yuika said.

I couldn't read the text, either, but the images had me convinced.

So it really was going to be like this after all. Wear the clothes in the treasure chest to advance onward, yup.

"But what would this be? This image shows people covered in water and protecting their chests with both arms," Gabby pointed out.

"There are x marks over their eyes, too, so it's probably just saying that there are traps, right…? Um, Takioto, what's going on? You're acting pretty suspicious."

"N-nothing."

"…You wouldn't happen to know the ancient language, would you?"

Yuika stared at me with reproach. What did I even do to tip her off? She was way too sharp.

But what was I supposed to do? The honest truth was that I couldn't advance onward without filling them both in. That said, I was reluctant to tell them absolutely everything.

"I—I can understand a little."

"Really?! Then what's this say?" Yuika asked, pointing toward the girl dressed up in the outfit from the chest. Next to it was a winding path.

"First, this isn't the end of the dungeon, apparently. It looks like we have to continue on a bit after this, but…"

"This snaking drawing has to be the corridor, then."

"Now then. This is just according to what's written here, mind you. Umm, the women need to wear these clothes or else it looks like we won't be able to move forward!"

After I said this, Yuika's expression changed from one of reproach to intimidation.

"Excuse me?"

"Y-Yuika, you really shouldn't give people scary looks."

"I mean, what do you expect, Takioto? Why don't you take a minute to really digest what you just said, okay? Why in the world do I need to wear a getup like this?"

"O-okay, just calm down a sec. I mean, I'd say it looks, er, really nice and liberating, wouldn't you agree?"

"Huuuuh?! Did your brains boil in your skull?! Okay then, go put on a super-high-waisted thong and tell me just how liberating and wonderful it is!"

"Just what sorta perverted stuff are you into?!"

"I literally just repeated what you said!"

"I—I mean, I only told you what was written here, that's all…and it seems we can't advance forward without wearing them… O-oh yeah, but check that out."

I pointed at the circle and square drawn on the wall.

"Put up excellent marks, and not only will you get a commemorative medal, but it also looks like you'll get an award certificate, too."

"What're you going on about? We're not at an athletic meet here! Who would even want that?! What the hell do 'excellent marks' even consist of anyway?!"

We were on the exact same page. Except in the game, the award certificate is a really precious item that's hard to part with. How could she possibly think about throwing it away?!

"Well, about that. It looks like there's going to be a lot of traps up ahead, so I'm guessing you get these excellent marks based on how well you can slip past them all…?"

"I—I get it. The picture of the girl covering her chest with both arms must be showing someone who stepped on a trap and is protecting themselves."

Almost, but not quite. You were right, Yuika, but you were still missing a little something. Gaaaaaaaaaah!

For any normal game filled with pretty girls, yeah, that would probably be the long and short of it. But this was an *eroge*. And not just any eroge. This was *Magical★Explorer*. There was no way it would just end there!

"…What are you writhing in agony over there for, Takioto?"

"Huh? Oh, um, well—"

"…Come with me a minute. Gabby, just sit there and wait for a second!"

Yuika grabbed my arm and returned with me to the previous floor, leaving Gabby grumbling there alone.

"Okay, Takioto. Spill it."

I was happy to get pushed up against the wall by a very cute girl, but my fear was winning out here. Still, I definitely felt a degree of pleasure.

"S-spill what?"

"You actually know something about this, don't you? I won't get mad; just lay it all out."

How'd she know?! I haven't said a damn thing!

As I tormented myself over what to do, a bit of a forlorn look abruptly came over Yuika, and she sighed.

"Listen, Takioto… You may not have noticed, but I'm really grateful for what you've done for me."

"Oh, well—"

"Sorry, just let me finish. I'm grateful, and at the same time, I trust you. Ludie, Yukine, and Nanami also seem to have put their faith in you. And you've done so much for me already."

Then Yuika brushed aside a lock of brown hair from her eyes, placed it behind her ear, and flashed me a childlike smile.

"Eventually…I'll open up to you about everything that's troubling me. You know what, I'll even tell you my three sizes. How about that?! So I want you to talk to me, too ♪!"

Huh?

"Th-thwee sizes?"

Where was this nonsense coming from?! Had she drank some weird medicine or something?

"Why're you talking like a baby all of a sudden? I'm just saying that to show you how resolved I am here, and I figured whatever you had to say was probably something sleazy like that. Geez, c'mon! Ohhh? Wait, Takioto, does that mean you're curious about my vital statistics?! Pervy, pervy Takioto's at it again ♪."

Stop poking your boobs with your finger like that!

Also, I'm sorry to say, Yuika, but I already know your three sizes.

Actually. Wait, how did she figure out I was hiding something lewd from her?! I didn't say anything to give her that idea, right?

Ah, forget it. At this point, it was better to just lay it all out on the table. But was it okay for something like *that*? But if I don't tell her, it'll be even more… *Aaaaaargh!*

I wasn't getting anywhere; I needed to take a deep breath.

Was it better to tell her or not? I could have just pretended not to know anything at all. Even if something happened, it wouldn't be life-threatening or anything, and honestly, all we had to do was take care not to fall down in the dungeon.

And since she'd managed to read into things this much, I didn't really have any choice but to talk, did I?

If anything happened, Yuika was all but assured to give me a cold stare. Though, I got the feeling she'd give me that same cold look when I told her what was coming up regardless.

Still, if she so desperately wanted me to confess everything like this, it would prove harder to keep it all secret.

"O-okay, fine. But I want you to keep your cool while I'm talking to you about it. Don't get mad, okay?"

"I won't! Besides, it's not like it's your fault anyway, Takioto."

That was true. I felt the same.

"R-right. Okey dokey, then... The truth is, what was written back there in the ancient language didn't just say to put on those clothes."

"I mean, I've gathered that much."

Yeaaaah, of course she had.

"With that in mind, do you remember that picture of the girl covered in water? Those traps will spray water on you when you trip them, but...that picture there shows what happens when you step on a trap and get sprayed."

"Huh, so that was actually showing someone covered in water, then."

How could I put this in the most delicate manner possible? I really wanted to sort of cushion the blow somehow to make it less of a bombshell. Water, water... What did water bring to mind?

Crap, I couldn't think up anything! Fine then, I'll take whatever. Just give me something to work with here!

"So you see, water is transparent, right?"

"...Where in the world is this going? Of course it is."

"And clothes, they're warm, right? That's why I think you'd want some that become see-through when you get them wet."

"You realize that everything you're saying is incoherent nonsense, right? Like there'd ever be something like that, please. Clothing you'd want to make transparent? Please, that's crazy...talk... Hmm? When they get... When they get...wet!"

"Th-the truth is, those clothes? Well, um, when you get water on them, they become totally see-through! Whoopsies!"

"...Whaaaaaaaaaaaaaaaaaaaat?!"

"G-get them wet, and they're one hundred percent see-through!"

Idiots, all of them, everyone who made this stupid game! It went without saying, but I reloaded my save file over and over again just to dive straight into some water and collect everyone's CGs. Yes, I admit it, I admit iiiiiiit!

"Are you kidding me?! What are clothes like that doing in a treasure chest?! Why do we have to wear them if we want to move on?!"

Just take a minute and think about it—of course a treasure chest would contain items to use during a lewd scene! And obviously, you have to put them on, right?! And it was natural to plunge into the water.

"Y-Yuika?"

She was trembling and looking at the ground, her hands balled into fists. I couldn't see what sort of face she was making, but she was red all the way to her ears.

"I—I get it now. So if you step on a trap, you'll be covered in water, and your chest will be on full display…! That's why the people in the diagram had their hands over their chests, yup, yup, suuuure!"

"S-sorry. Lemme just say one thing: This isn't my fault!"

"I totally get that, all right?!"

If there was anyone to blame here, it was the developers! It was certainly not my fault, but the truth was that eroge players were looking for a lewd scene after these sorts of boss battles. The developers understood this and were just trying to meet their players' expectations, sure, but it wasn't like us eroge players had tried to butt in or anything! Whatever the case, the developers had undeniably slipped in the erotic scene.

So it was all their fault!! Exceeeeept I really couldn't explain that to Yuika, could I?!

Anyway, it was impossible to escape reality! I needed to follow up with something here, some sort of pro to mitigate the con of putting on see-through magical-girl clothes…!

Th-that's it! There was still something after all!

"H-hold on a second. There's still a bright side. If you manage to get through here without getting sprayed with water once, you get a sweet commemorative medal *and* an award certificate. How about that?!"

"Whoo-hoo, a certificate, lucky me! Like hell I'd want something like that! I need that about as much as I need a leg of a centipede! And all that stuff about 'excellent marks' on that diagram back there—that's about not getting sprayed, is it?!"

"Centipede leg" was going way too far! It's still an award certificate, you know?! Though, when you compared an "award certificate" with a "sexy CG you could get by spraying water over a girl," a stupid certificate was practically the same value as a bug leg! So I guess they really are worthless?!

"*Uuuuuugh!* Yup, fine, I get it!!"

"Y-you got it?"

"I've made up my mind. I'll wear it."

"Huh?"

"I'll wear it! I'll wear it, all right?! I'll put it on and charge ahead. I just need to avoid getting sprayed at all costs, right?" she said, grabbing my collar. Her face was still beet red, and her eyes were burning with resolve as her lips quivered.

The outrageous conversation had gone on so long that I got the feeling Yuika was forgetting the fact that those magical-girl clothes were already pretty sexy and risqué themselves. But pointing that out would only make things worse, so I kept my mouth shut.

"Let's...not tell Gabby all this. There's no telling what will happen," Yuika said.

Was I the only one here who thought something bad would happen whether we told her or not?

"Please don't say anything. Okay, I'm going to call Gabby. We're going to go change over there. Stay here until I call you, got it?" she said before taking her hands off me, twirling around, and walking away.

I hastily called out to her as I watched her leave.

"Hold up. Are you seriously okay with this?! If anything happens..."

Don't you realize it's all going to be on display?!

"Either way, we need to wear them if we want to move on, right? Besides—"

She turned around, slowly came back to me, and placed her forehead up against my chest.

"—even if I do step on a trap...you'll put your body on the line to protect me, won't you?"

"...O-of course I will!"

"I knew it! Okay, time to get changed!"

As she bounced over to the spatial magic circle, she abruptly stopped in her tracks. Then with her back still turned, she called out my name.

"What is it?"

"Um, well. I just thought I better tell you something."

"Tell me what?"

"Any other guy and I'd absolutely hate it, but if it's you, Takioto...I wouldn't mind if you got a little peek."

Then she stepped into the magic circle.

The *Magical★Explorer* developers were truly wonderful people who deserved to be lauded far and wide.

Generally for eroge or other fan-service games, developers would devote a lot of resources to sexy and erotic scenes, though they also made sure to polish the story and characters.

The players wanted these scenes, so it was fair to say they *had* to put a lot of effort into them.

The developers of *Magical★Explorer* were of course no exception, and they made no compromises when they created *that* scene. The same was true for the setup.

When I first played this part of the game, I was gripped by both anxiety and anticipation. I was worried that one of the heroines would say something like *Can't we just wear these on top of our clothes?*

But the devs must have anticipated a loophole like this, because they seemed to have thought of everything in this scene. This was evident in lines such as:

"Wearing magical-girl clothes over the skin imbues the outfits with mana, which automatically unlocks barriers throughout the dungeon."

As well as:

"Wearing clothing over the magical-girl outfits prevents them from radiating mana, keeping the barriers up and making it impossible to move forward."

They exhaustively shoved in so much extra setup, and the heroines all try to see if they can cheat the system somehow, but each and every attempt ends in failure. The scene that shows them taking off their second layer of clothes, their faces red with humiliation after hitting a wall, is truly fantastic.

Indeed. The game allowed me to enjoy seeing all manner of reactions from the heroines, from those who huddled into a ball after being forced into the outfit, to others who quivered in shame, and still others who would readily grab a wand and strike a pose in the getup.

*   *   *

That was why I had thought I needed to laud the devs.

But now I wanted to "laud" them straight to hell!

How many more times were they going to back me into a corner like this before they were satisfied? I mean, just think about it a second—having to equip sexy equipment in order to proceed? Turning clothes totally see-through when they get wet? Try experiencing that in real life for yourself! It may have seemed like nothing but a bonus in the game, but dealing with it in real life feels like straight up torture, assholes! You know *I'm* the one who has to ask that they do all this, right?!

"Guess it won't work after all..."

"We've been blocked by an invisible wall," Yuika said while she placed her clothes in her storage bag. She was wearing the magical-girl outfit in question, but for some reason, she stood confident and imposing.

Open sides, accentuated breasts, thighs in a miniskirt. The holy trinity all in a single outfit—I was compelled to give the devs my highest gratitude for coming up with it.

"You look like you're totally fine with this, Yuika."

"Oh, please, what're you talking about? This is just pure desperation, that's it. Listen, Takioto. Do you know what you have to do in times like these? Just shrug it all off! Feeling ashamed only makes the embarrassment worse!" she said before glancing over at Gabby. I followed her and looked over at the girl.

"I cannot believe that...I've been forced into such a shameful outfit...! *Hngh!*"

Gabby was pulling down on her skirt, trembling.

She must have noticed I was looking at her, because she bashfully tried to hide herself with her hands.

Between the two of them, I think Yuika was handling it the right way. Still, it was incredible that she was able to put that kind of thinking into practice. However, I had noticed that Yuika's face was pink, and her hands were shaking slightly.

She noticed my stare, and her face grew even redder as she glared hard at me. An idea must have come to her, because she put some space between us and grinned.

"Well, go on. What do you think? Does it look good on me?" she asked as she grabbed the hem of her skirt, twirling around in place.

Once she was done, she put her foot out in front of her and started to briefly flip up her skirt, the hem pinched between her fingers. I could almost… Nope, I couldn't get a glimpse.

So listen.

Could she quit it with stuff like this? Despite how I may have looked, I was a sensible gentleman, and it took every fiber of my being to feign composure while chanting the Heart Sutra in my head in the face of such obscene behavior.

Didn't she get it? I was devoting everything I had to sealing away my consciousness, and she wanted me to compliment her? She was asking the impossible here!

Yuika wanted to know if it looked good on her, did she?

Of course it did. If anything, it looked *too* good on her! It looked so damn good, I was losing my mind. *Hwoooooooooaaaaaaaaah!*

Oh yeah, and Yuika, why the hell were you picking up your skirt and flipping it ever so slightly up like that that?! It was already racy enough— how dumb can you get? You were going to get me arrested for breaking and entering that absolute territory!

Also, one more thing—what the hell was with those healthy, cultured, over-the-top thigh-highs of yours? They're too damn naughty, that's for sure!

"Come oooon, Takioto. Tell me, what do you think?"

My mind was about ready to break here.

No, no, this wasn't good. I had to calm myself down. Those were just daikon radishes, yup, just radishes, uh-huh.

Daikon with just a little bit of plumpness to them—porcelain white, silky smooth, and very soft-looking. They probably smelled great, and I would have loved to place my face between them. Oh, and I bet they would look good in tights, but on second thought, maybe knee-highs would look… Wait, we're not talking about radishes at all here!!

Dammit, okay, calm down… She already thinks you're a hopeless horndog as it is. Be cool, be cool, be cool. I didn't want to give her an even weirder impression of me than she already had! There was no need to rack my brain for the right words here. I just had to reply with something simple, cool, and chivalrous, that was it! Simple, cool, chivalrous.

"Hmmm, pretty hot, I'd say."

AAAAAAAAAAGH!

What the hell did I just say?! That was laying my lust right on the damn table!

"Awww, c'mon now, what's with that weak, half-hearted reaction? Doesn't this make you happy?"

Hold up a damn minute, everything worked out fine?! She thought I just said the first thing that popped into my head?! Well, all righty then, we'll go with that.

"I'm just kidding, it looks great on you. It looks just as great on you, too, Gabby. Super cute."

"Riiiight?"

"...O-of course it does."

The way Gabby tried to act tough despite being so embarrassed was perfectly sublime.

The fact that she looked slimmer in clothing was just fantastic, too. The places that stuck out really stuck out properly, and she had a seductive physique similar to Sis's. I wanted to be enveloped in her.

Now, that was all well and good, but the problem lay in the clothes' unique property.

I hadn't told Gabby that they'd turn transparent if they got wet. I wondered what would happen if I mentioned it. Worst case, we wouldn't be able to take a single step forward, maybe? I mean, as long as she didn't get any water on her, she'd never know.

It was simple; I just needed to put my body on the line to protect the two of them. It didn't make any difference to me if I was wet or not. As much as I would have loved to see the two of them drenched, I obviously couldn't let that happen.

"Okay, let's head out."

At my words, Yuika marched forward energetically, making big strides, while Gabby took tiny steps in the same direction. She was still embarrassed, by the look of things.

I followed behind the both of them and tried to close in on the magic circle. Then it happened.

I bumped into something invisible.

"Huh?"

It didn't hurt, nor was there any impact. I simply couldn't advance beyond that spot.

"What's wrong, Takioto?"

The two of them looked at me with confusion. They both seemed to be on the other side of this invisible wall, though…

"Oh, it's just, there seems to be this invisible wall here?"

I punched the area in front of me with my Third Hand as hard as I could.

However, my Third Hand also got stuck at that same point. It didn't even make a sound when it stopped.

"Hmm? An invisible wall…? I just passed by there… Ah!"

Yuika suddenly raised her voice and looked at me. After checking herself out, she glanced at Gabby this time before turning her gaze back on me.

Gabby followed suit and looked at everyone one by one. Then just like Yuika, she cried, "Oh my!" and stared at the treasure chest.

"Oh…"

I couldn't help but vocalize my reaction.

I took in the magical-girl clothes that Gabby and Yuika were pulling off extremely well, then at the third magical-girl outfit lying on top of the chest, before glancing back at my clothes.

Unfortunately, that was when everything came together.

"Whaaaaat?!"

"Takiooootooo, what's wrong? You reeeeeally shouldn't stare at other people with that face you have on right now!"

"I mean, what do you expect? Just think about it for a minute, Yuika. Why do I have to wear something like that?"

"*P-pfft!* But it looks so nice and liberating, doesn't it?"

"Youuuuuu little! How dare you throw my words back in my face right now?! I apologize, I take it all back, I'm sorry!"

"The roles have been reversed, it would seem…"

"Whew, booooy, who's the pervert now, hmm ♪?"

"What the hell do you look so damn pleased about?!"

All right, I wanted whoever thought up this stupid setup to come out here and rub their forehead on the floor this damn instant! Who the hell'd even want to cosplay as a magical girl and try clearing this wet and wild dungeon for perverts, dammit?!

"It's okay, Takioto! Put up excellent marks, and not only will you get a commemorative medal, but it also looks like you'll get an award certificate, too!"

"I'm sorry! You have my most heartfelt apologies, so please, no more!"

"I don't really need you to say sorry or anything. Now then, let's get you out of those clothes!"

Whoa, whoa, whoa now, hold up here.

"Hey, why're you coming over here with those grubby mitts? W-wait, please. I need some mental prep time, pleas— Hey, why're you also touching me, Gabby? I can get myself changed just fine, so stop— Hey— Nooooooo!"

Let me ask you, have you ever overcome something before?

Ever toil and suffer to break through?

I...exchanged something very important of mine to do just that.

Ahh, why was it? I wondered. The wall that hadn't budged an inch after I slammed my Third Hand into it so hard seemed like it had never been there in the first place as I passed through.

But still, I wished someone would tell me it was all a mistake.

That I wasn't dressed up in a magical-girl outfit.

Magical girls were like a dream, so to speak, the kind that sent young girls in elementary school and older adult men into a frenzy. I saw them as a kind of holy ground.

Wearing a magical outfit like this gave me strangely mixed feelings, like I had forever defiled a sacred place yet also like my mind was being cleansed by becoming one with such a sanctuary.

The best way to describe it was that I had been reborn.

I was currently inside a dark and damp dungeon, sure, but I felt as if I was lying down in a wide-open field, my arms spread out.

I didn't have anything to fear anymore.

"*Pff-pfft*, y-you look g-great, Takioto," Yuika said.

"Really?"

"Y-yes, quite so, *pfft*, um, yes. It complements you much more than I expected, *pfft*!"

Et tu, Gabby?

I wouldn't let those trivial things bother me right now.

"Ahh, what a wonderful breeze."

"Uh, we're still in a dungeon here; are you so happy that it's broken you?"

"It almost seems like he's become enlightened, does it not? Takioto, are you all right?"

"I'm fine. The whole world is sparkling ★."

"Yeaaah, I think we've lost him. I have a wig with me right now; do you want to put it on him?"

"...A wonderful suggestion."

Could they stop leaving me behind and trying to level up my cross-dressing game here? Better yet, why the hell were they chatting together like normal? Had forcing me into women's clothing brought them into an alliance or something?

"Come on then, look sharp!" Yuika said.

"I mean, I'm not really feeling it, you know?"

"All right, then why don't you strike a cool pose? Nanami said it herself—striking a pose pulls mind and body together."

Just what sort of world had Nanami and Yuika envisioned in their conversations? I would think that they were grounded in a lot more common sense than the ones Nanami talked about with Sis.

"I have a tripod with me, so let's take a picture, shall we? I actually borrowed this from Nanami."

"You really want to leave proof of your shameful past behind...?"

"At first, it was really embarrassing, but now it's just sorta fun. Besides, don't you want to get a look at your entire body, Takioto?"

I had to admit that I was grimly curious. But hold on, she mentioned borrowing the tripod from Nanami, but what were the circumstances that led up to that happening?

And why was Gabby posing with a magic wand in her hands? She had been embarrassed to death just a few moments ago. Had seeing me cross-dress really quelled her shame that significantly?

"Okay, Takioto. You get the most important spot, right in the middle. Since you're over there, Gabby, I'll stand on the opposite side."

"Should I perhaps raise my arm up a bit higher?"

"Right about there should be just fine!"

It was really hard to object to all this when the two of them were talking in a friendly-ish manner. Since when had they gotten so chummy? Either something happened while they were changing or while I was changing. Where had all the bickering gone?

...They were *really* enjoying themselves as they talked, huh.

Guess it was time to steel myself.

"Fine, fine, I just need to pose, right?! Okay, okay, I'll pose, dammit!"

Standing next to Gabby, who was already in position, I dropped my hips, put my hand on my katana, and got ready to draw it.

Yuika set her Tsukuyomi Traveler on the tripod and put something on my head when she came over to us. This was...

"A wig?"

"Make sure to stay nice and still, okay?! Let's have your hair fall this way."

Her white arms smoothly reached up to my head. She was grabbing my hair and neatening it out, but she hadn't forgotten, had she? She realized these magical-girl outfits had open sides, right?

If she showed me those pale, beautiful, and mystically immoral armpits of hers, my body, or rather, my heart was going to go haywire.

Yup. Stuffing the remaining two magical-girl outfits in my item bag had definitely been the right call.

"*Tee-hee*, peeeerfect! All right, time for pictures."

Then Yuika went around behind me and chirped, "Say cheese!"

When later I looked at the picture, it hit me.

A dark and embarrassing piece of my past had just been born.

I managed to erase the memory and continued into the magic circle.

Just like before, the same cave-style dungeon continued on...or at least, I wished that was the case.

"How pretty..."

Water flowed out from the brick walls, and an inch or so of water flowed along the floor. It was all too clear that it had come to kill us.

This was a floor with a huge number of traps, too. Unfortunately, all of them were max-level traps that my ring was unable to detect.

Dammit, why hadn't Iori been blocked by that invisible wall in the game? It wasn't shown in any of the pictures, but was there a microscopic possibility that he had been wearing magical-girl clothes, too? Honestly, I wanted to see it myself.

It had been just as unexpected with Nanami, now that I thought about it. Back then, there had been options that didn't exist in the game... and while I tried not to think that everything would be exactly like it had been in-game, I might not have been conscious enough of that fact. It was just some clothes, though, and I hadn't made some sort of fatal mistake in an event or anything.

Nevertheless, I had sustained a devastating mental wound.

The one saving grace, however, was that I was able to keep my stole equipped. The dungeon must have considered it a weapon? They could try spraying water at me from any direction, but I'd defend everyone from all angles with lightning speed.

Except if I tried covering my body and hiding in my stole, I'd still get stopped by those invisible walls. Maybe there was some sort of mana being radiating around the clothes? I'm sure Sexy Scientist may have been able to understand that sort of stuff, but it was beyond me. I had finished most of the preparations, so I needed to go pay her a visit soon, huh.

But really, if I wasn't able to block any water, the other two would end up having a wardrobe malfunction while I'd be a walking broadcast accident. I had to do something, no matter what.

Time to fire myself up and concentrate.

"Oh, and what would that be?" Gabby said, and I followed where she was looking. For whatever reason, there was something extending from the stone-built dungeon's ceiling; they were like the streamers that popped out from a hanging party ball. Clearly suspicious.

Then Gabby began to walk toward it.

"Wait, wait, wait, wait!"

"Stop, Gabby, stop!"

"What? Don't worry, I was not going to pull on it, of course."

While I agreed she might not have pulled it on purpose, in Gabby's case, I could clearly imagine her stumbling right in front of it and tugging down on the thread.

"Takioto! I've got a really bad feeling all of a sudden…!"

"Really?!"

"Yeah, my intuition's telling me that area's bad news."

If that was Yuika's gut reaction, then there was no doubt.

I swiftly searched through my belongings and took out a low-level earth sigil stone. Aiming for the area around the thread, I activated the stone.

When I did, a magic circle rose up in front of me, and from it flew a stone about the size of a person's head. It then smashed into the ground next to the thread. Water instantly shot up from below.

The liquid quickly died down, but there had been more than enough of it to soak us through.

"What is the idea here, I wonder? It is just some water. Does the dungeon think this would be enough to stop us?"

"...Wh-what a dastardly trap."

"O-oookay, this is seriously messed up, isn't it?! It was aiming precisely at our most dangerous areas."

Sorry, Gabby. I understand why you're looking at us with furrowed eyes and all, but I can't tell you anything.

More importantly, though, this trap. Yuika was absolutely right that it was aimed with precision at a dangerous place—the lower body. Of course, you always aimed for the vitals during combat, but it was absolute madness to set a trap like that in a random corridor.

"Planning on finishing us off in one shot, huh."

"T-Takioto? We've only just gotten here, right? This is way too lethal right out of the gate."

I thought so, too. Faking us out with the thread and shooting up from below, instead. And *this* was the very first one?!

I needed to shift my focus elsewhere. Concentrate. I needed to concentrate. I needed to remember that time I was meditating under the waterfall. At the time, Yukine looked phenomenal, all dressed up as a shrine maiden and soaked in the wat— No, no, no, no! My mind was wandering off course.

Right now, I *really* couldn't let myself think about that stuff. I needed to protect myself, protect the two of them.

"What in heaven's name has gotten into you two...? Forget it, let us continue forward," Gabby said before starting to proceed ahead.

"Hold on a second here, Gabby! There's something important I need to tell you."

I quickly took her hand and pulled her back toward me. Then with a short, deep breath, I expelled the wicked thoughts in my head.

"I don't know what you think of me, but I consider both you and Yuika to be very important friends."

"H-huh?! Wh-what did you say?!"

"I want to protect you, and right now, I'm trying to do just that."

Gabby stared at me with a blank look of confusion.

When I brought her hand up to my chest, she stared back at me in befuddlement.

"The thing is, I don't want you to get hurt."

Indeed, I didn't want her to experience such mental anguish. I felt it wholeheartedly. Still, I didn't know what Gabby was going to do. The worst-case possibility was that she might get Yuika and me wrapped up in this somehow. That was why...

"This place is dangerous. So I'll lead the charge. You should follow behind me. No matter what happens, I'll protect you."

The least she could do was get behind me. Don't do anything weird. Please—

—let these feelings of mine reach her.

"Okay...!"

Nodding slightly, I looked at her and let go of her hand. Then I glanced at Yuika to signal us to move ahead, but she had her mouth half-open in a gasp of disgust.

"What's wrong, Yuika?"

"Oh, it's nothing. Nothing at all."

"You should stay near my stole, too. Worst-case scenario, I'll act as a shield."

I was probably the one who'd suffer the lightest damage from having my clothes drenched and turned see-through. It'd just put my mind on life support, that was all. I absolutely didn't want things to end up like that, and I was going to do my best to make sure it didn't.

"If you feel anything, tell me immediately. I'm trusting you. Let's all get through this together!"

I was going to use everything at my disposal. If needed, I'd use my sigil stones, earth or otherwise, no problem. I wasn't going to *need* them much anyway, save for one section. This wasn't the time to be acting stingy.

From there, we continued on with the maximum amount of caution possible, but in what was perhaps contrary to our expectations, we had a pretty smooth time of it. That was thanks to Yuika and Gabby.

Yuika could detect dangerous areas and tell us ahead of time, and Gabby could use long-ranged magic to attack and investigate any suspicious places.

Part of me was even worried that I was the one contributing the least here this time.

However, there was always the chance that this smooth sailing was making us drop our guard. We couldn't lose concentration here.

"Hold on, what do you think that is?"

I stopped them both and pointed to the chest sitting alone in the corridor. It differed from the chest with the magical-girl clothes. More importantly, though, it was a luxurious chest.

Seeing it, Gabby's eyes lit up. However, Yuika wore a solemn expression.

"Wh-why, it's a treasure chest!"

"So that's a trap, then…!"

"Yup, it's definitely a trap, all right…!"

Gabby glared at us with her once-sparkling eyes.

"Now, hold on, Gabby. I get why you're excited, I really do."

I got just as happy when I discovered a treasure chest myself. However, I wanted her to recall the first thing that happened when we entered this floor.

It tried taking a snipe at our lower body, right?

"Water might shoot out the moment we open it."

"If that is all, then I don't really see what the problem could be."

"That's not it, Takioto, you got to think a bit more twisted than that. Earlier, the thread itself was a fake-out. Perhaps the treasure is just a fake-out this time, too. "

"…Fair."

I was careless. The objective here was to make us concentrate on the chest. In that case…

"Gabby, I want you to do something for me. Can you shoot some magic near the treasure chest?"

With reluctance, she cast a spell. The instant Gabby's proficient light magic, in the form of light bullets this time, hit the wall next to the treasure chest, a strong jet of water shot out.

So the treasure itself was the real trap after all.

"I'm really glad to have you with us, Gabby. I can continue forward with peace of mind knowing I have someone so reliable at my back."

"…I-is that so, now? I have sort of mixed feelings about that."

"No, Takioto, it's still too early to be relieved. Take a look over there."

I stared hard where Yuika pointed. There, I saw something with the head of a fish…

"Carplins?"

Carplins referred to a monster that looked like a combination of a goblin and a fish, and it was impossible to properly describe how weak they were. The last time I'd come across them was in the Beginner's Dungeon.

They were weaker than the blue and squishy slimes in a certain nationally beloved RPG series, so weak that it was rude to even compare the two. Any attack this thing launched at us probably wasn't going to damage us at all. Physically anyway.

However, right here and right now, this weakling possessed the most high-powered attack of all. They were such pitiful monsters, if anything, I started to think they had only been created for this exact purpose.

Their favorite attack was a water gun. It just made you wet and did almost no damage. The only thing to really worry about was that it might make you slip and fall down.

But right now? Their jets of water had the potential to graze our dangerous areas. Putting it lightly, the wound would be fatal.

However, they weren't supposed to have much health. A single punch from Yuika or me would be able to kill one. But there wasn't just one of them. There were multiple. The slightest misstep, and we could be heading straight for a broadcast-blooper situation.

"Let's hide for now."

They must have picked up on something. One of the carplins was acting strange, so I shot Yuika a look. Next, pulling Gabby with me, we all hid behind a protruding boulder.

Then I heard the splashing footsteps of the carplin.

"Carrr, carrr, carrr, carrr, carrr."

I assumed it was saying something along the lines of *Huuuh, that sure is weird*.

As I watched the carplin head back with splattering footsteps, I sighed.

"What're we going to do?"

"Nobody told me we were going to run into such a powerful foe here."

"…You looked so calm and composed battling the Rotting Hellhound earlier, so why are mere *carplins* all of a sudden such a problem?" Gabby grumbled.

"That's not the point," I said to her, shaking my head. "If they manage to snag us in a bad spot, they'll inflict wounds that even healing magic can't mend."

"That only makes me even more confused," Gabby said.

"What're we going to do?"

"Fortunately, they still haven't noticed our presence. It's a straight corridor, and we have to get past them somehow. Should we pelt them with everything we've got?"

"Hard, instantaneous annihilation—let's do it. We're counting on you, Gabby!"

"Yes, yes, I get it...," she replied. She began casting a spell, and Yuika and I prepared to leap into action. I sent mana into my stole so I could immediately pound the carplins into dust.

Yuika didn't have her gauntlet equipped, but she could pulverize one of those creatures with a single punch.

"Here I go!"

Right as Gabby's light bullet shot from the magic circle, Yuika and I jumped out from behind the rock.

The light bullet hit one of the carplins head-on and sent it flying. No way they were surviving that. Four left. I immediately opened up my stole and punched one of the carplins away.

I kept going and slammed another carplin into the air before turning to look at Yuika.

She was also in the midst of defeating two of the monsters herself.

But she hadn't noticed. The color at her feet was slightly off.

"Crap!"

The sound of a splash. Followed by Yuika's scream.

Thankfully, I had acted immediately. She was on her hands and knees, but she was safe. It wasn't new information, but she was wearing white.

"A-aah..."

Yuika looked at me in panic. I didn't have a choice. The water slowly soaked deeper and deeper, and my shoulder gradually became more exposed.

"T-Takioto...! Y-you protected me...!"

"Oh, c'mon now, this is just a scra—"

"Don't try to act tough... Your eyes are rolling back into your head!"

"T-Takioto! What happened?"

"Ah, Gabby. You saw, did you?"

Saw me, with everything from my shoulder to one side of my chest on full display.

Realizing the danger of her own outfit, she hugged her body as fear overtook her.

"It's okay, Gabby. Just calm down. I'll apologize for not saying anything. But you have to believe me; I didn't mean to keep it a secret. I just thought it would be better if I didn't tell you."

She glared at me while on the verge of tears, slowly tottering backward until she hit the wall and then—the sound of a *click*.

"Look out!"

Water shot out from a hole in the wall. I spread my stole out and protected Gabby. However.

"A-ahhhh! T-Takioto!"

I wasn't able to protect myself. It appeared this trap was set to aim at the chest, each one of the damn things going right for the proverbial jugular.

"I told you, didn't I, Gabby? That I'd protect you?"

"But, Takioto, your nipples..."

"They're definitely hard... Aroused, are we?"

"Hey, c'mon, you two. What're you making that face for? It's fine, I may have ended up looking like this, but I kept you both dry. So go ahead and stare."

Witness me.

"Yuika, follow along behind me once you've determined it's safe. I'm leaving Gabby in your hands."

"T-Takioto? Wh-what are you planning to do?"

"I'm going to clear a path," I said before rushing off. It was pure desperation at this point. Screw these traps, I just needed to activate every last one to get outta here, right?!

Tripping trap after trap, I tried to dodge the water flying at me in every direction as much as could. I forged wholeheartedly ahead, running ever forward, while also pulverizing the occasional carplin that showed up along the way.

Fortunately, we were already close to the finish line. It didn't take long for the spatial magic circle to come into view. When I came to a stop, I timidly checked my body. My consciousness threatened to leave me, but I managed to stand firm and turn back behind me.

Seeing the two girls in their pretty magical-girl outfits made it feel real.

I had managed to protect them. I was filled with a bubbling sense of accomplishment, along with a strange sense of liberation.

"Look there, it's the spatial magic circle!"

At my nod, Yuika and Gabby both dashed toward the magic circle. They looked so happy.

It happened right as they were about to reach the circle—Gabby stumbled on something, fell down, and there was a loud *click*. The instant I heard it, I immediately filled my stole with mana. The site of my final trial would be mere steps from our exit.

As I listened to the deafening rumble, totally unlike the trap sounds up until now, I glanced cautiously in every direction.

Where was it going to come from? Up? Down? Left? Right? The front? The back…? It was from behind… A huge amount of…a massive… No, no, please, no!

"O-oh no, oh no, oh no, oh no, oh no!"

"Wh-what're we supposed to do about this?!"

What the heck was up with all that water? They really saved the absolute largest one for last, didn't they? Were they trying to make a pool here, or…? Hmmm. Nope, this was impossible.

"We just need to make a break for the magic cir— Oh, welp, now we're trapped in some weird cage."

It was too late. I dispersed the mana I had sent into my stole.

Y'know, I'd really given it my all. Even put my own body on the line and everything.

But honestly, I had sort of known from the start that it was going to end up like this.

I mean, this was Gabby, after all. Yup, *the* Gabby. The one and only.

Ah, but she was so cute as she panicked with tears in her eyes. This truly was where Gabby shone the most, wasn't it? Don't worry, Yuika. You won't physically die here, just socially.

"Takiotooo! Don't give up now! Hurry up and make a wall for us!"

"Nah, it's just too much."

With that, we were engulfed by water.

I heard splashing. I opened my eyes to discover I had fallen down on my back. It appeared that I'd been washed away, but there was no way to tell just how far I had gone.

Needless to say, my body was drenched, and my outfit was totally transparent. This would get me banned from any and every video-upload site out there or get hidden by the little guy with the sign they used in anime. Don't look!

"Where are Gabby and Yuika…?"

I looked around me and made out a lone female figure lying on the ground. That back, that big butt, and that blond hair, I guess. It was Gabby. That ass had to belong to Gabby.

"*Unh…unghh…*"

"Gabb—"

I was about to call to her when I stopped. I thought it best to relax a minute and take in the sight of Gabby's butt.

It was *totally* soaked through.

She was in the same immodest state that I was in. Though she was fortunate to have landed facedown, with her back exposed, I'd still gotten a full, X-ray vision–style view of it.

But where was Yuika? I couldn't spot her anywhere nearby.

Carplins would have been the only monsters that appeared here, so the physical danger was negligible. But when I considered the worst-case scenario, I decided it would be better to find her as soon as possible.

Suppressing my urge to flip Gabby over, I took out my spare stole. As reluctant I was to part from the beautiful behind, I covered her with it before shaking her.

"C'mon, Gabby. Wake up, Gabby!"

"*Uuuhn, mhnnnn.* Takioto, that is dog food you have there…"

What the heck was she dreaming about? Forget it, I needed her to wake up fast.

I shook her body again. Finally, she came to.

"Oh, Takioto… *Eek!*"

She was awake.

"Oh, sorry."

And when she got up.

"N-not at all, that wasn't my intention. I certainly didn't shove you away out of ill will. I, um, I just—"

Shooting up to her feet in a panic wasn't the right move. The stole I placed over Gabby slid down to the ground.

"Ah!"

Jaw-dropping.

Her boobs, her belly button, even down there. But her boobs! It was all breasts on full display. Crap, the stimulation was too strong. My titstilated mind was boobified. I couldn't tell if I could speak Japanese at this point or not.

"Eh? ...*Hnnnnh?!*"

At last Gabby noticed her current state, and her face turned redder than a lobster. Then she held her body tight in an attempt to cover herself with her hands and turned around.

"D-don't look at me!"

At this moment, Gabby shared something in common with the Venus de Milo.

The Venus de Milo had always been a beautiful statue, but it was famous for not having any arms. However, I had heard people claim that her lack of limbs stirred the viewer's imagination and heightened the magnificence of the piece.

In that regard, Gabby's clothes were totally see-through, so that everything was on full display yet not *entirely* visible. But Gabby grew even more beautiful when you imagined what those hidden areas might have contained. In other words.

The Venus de Milo equaled stirring the imagination, which equaled Gabby, who then meant Venus, ergo godly.

QED.

Gaaaaaaah, what dumbass nonsense was I thinking here?! Just calm down a minute...

Sheesh, Gabby really could be such a scatterbrain, huh? She turned around and crouched down, but all that did was emphasize that perfectly sculpted butt of hers! *Aaaaaaaah*, dammit, this absolutely ruuuuuuuuuuuuuuuuuuuuuuled!

Crouched on the floor was a haughty, drill-haired, pampered daughter of nobility in a magical-girl outfit, her face beet red. What the hell was I supposed to do if she feebly begged me not to look despite the drops of water smoothly dripping down her butt? If I tried to hold myself back any longer, I was going to have a damn brain hemorrhage, okay?!

Calm down, calm down. Think back to the situation at hand here. We were inside a dungeon.

On top of that, I still didn't have any idea where Yuika was or what she was up to. I had to do something. Wait...this current scene in front of me was kind of awful, huh? If we didn't know what was going on with Yuika, then she must not know what was going on with us, right? If she happened to try to come find us, uhh...

I glanced over at Gabby.

Gabby, her face flushed red, hugging herself close on the verge of tears, and me, staring at her. If Yuika saw us like this, her opinion of me was going to drop straight down to the bottom of the Mariana Trench. I just needed to do something before she saw us and—

"Takiooooto, Gaaaaaabby? Where are youuuu?! If you haven't been mentally broken yet, then say something!"

Ah, please, God. Grant me your salvation.

It was a good thing that my stole had been on the ground near Gabby. Putting two and two together, Yuika simply said, "Aren't you lucky?" so my life in society didn't come to an end. However, my spirit had been so worn down that it was on the verge of disappearing.

But hang on. Was "lucky" referring to the fact that I hadn't wound up getting punched or that I'd gotten a real spicy feast for the eyes?

"Looks like we've finally made it back."

Fortunately, or unfortunately, our outfits quickly dried off with fire and wind magic.

In all honesty, I would have loved to enjoy my fill of their drenched and see-through forms, but that obviously wasn't going to happen.

"What's that pervy face for? You must be thrilled. Did you get a nice look?"

Oh yeah, I saw quite a boo—a bunch, quite a bunch.

"W-well, if I had to say one way or the other, then yes, I got a peek. Hey, wait, what do you mean 'pervy face'?"

C'mon now, who wouldn't peek?

"*Ugh, you're the worst*…is what I'd like to say, but this time, there really wasn't much you could've done about it."

Gabby had an awfully conflicted look on her face. It was still slightly pink.

"In quite high spirits, aren't we?"

"Refreshed and invigorated, aren't we?"

"I mean, yeah, of course. Not just me, either, but you both, too, right?" I replied, and Gabby nodded.

"Um, Takioto…"

"What's up?"

"You have truly done so very much for me this day. If there is perhaps anything I can do for you, I implore you to say so. I will do anything you wish."

"I wouldn't say 'anything' to him if I were you. But I want to do something to thank you, too, Takioto. Anything you have in mind?"

Ah, Yuika was referring to the last time I helped her, huh? But when faced with the question…

"There's not really anything I can think of…"

"Whaaat, really, nothing? Isn't there something you want to eat or something we can buy you? Something we can do for you?"

"Hmmm, well, if I had to say *something*…"

I mulled it over and blurted out the first thought that came to mind.

It was probably this wet and wild dungeon that was to blame. I had been too wound up in there. That was why my heart felt so open and free.

Which then led to me inadvertently allowing my true thoughts to slip out. Thoughts that I never would have let pass my lips under normal circumstances. Thoughts that I had kept hidden this whole time.

A wish that couldn't be granted, but that, from the depths of my soul, I wanted to come true.

"It'd be real swell to hear you call me your 'big bro,' too… Oh, crap…"

Then I lost all sense of time.

Chapter 9 ⟨ **Each of Their Paths**   Magical★Explorer ⟩

Reborn as a Side Character in a Fantasy Dating Sim

—*Yuika's Perspective*—

"Come on in, Yuika, Gabriella, and Takioto," President Monica said with a cheery smile.

Takioto commented that there were almost as few people as were usually in the Ceremonial Committee, and the president muttered:

"Hmmm, apparently, something written in the ancient language popped up when Iori was clearing a dungeon…and his face went pale when he realized how dire things could potentially become. I'm expecting a detailed update in the near future, but it's got something to do with the library."

"I see," Takioto mumbled in reply. But something about his demeanor was strange.

"To what do I owe the pleasure? If I had to guess…it involves induction in the Three Committees, doesn't it?"

It made sense that Monica would assume as much when two people previously approached by the Student Council showed up at her door.

"Student Council President Monica, may I ask you to indulge me for a moment?" Gabby asked before looking me in the eyes and nodding.

"Indulge? Sure, go ahead. I'm listening."

"I previously declined the Student Council's invitation to join your ranks. If perhaps there is still an opening, however, would you extend me the same offer once again?"

"…Can you tell me what made you change your mind? Oh, it's not because I'm mad or anything. I'm just surprised, is all."

The president probably figured Gabby was going to join the Ceremonial Committee. I had thought so, too.

"I have made it this far by incessantly chasing after my older brother. But thanks to Takioto and Yuika, I've realized something: I am my own person. I wish to grow stronger in a way that suits me. Not by imitating him, but by heading down my own path to become as magnificent as he is."

"...So Benito's your goal, is he?"

"Indeed, I...I have always been following in Brother's footsteps. I believed that was the correct thing to do."

"But now it's not the right thing to do—is that what you're saying?"

"Yes. I want to surpass him. Instead of aiming for his heights at his side, I've realized I wish to find my own way of rising above him."

Then Gabby stared straight into President Monica's eyes, puffing out her chest, and said squarely:

"That is why I would like to join the Student Council."

"*Tee-hee, hee-hee-hee.*"

President Monica laughed. A sincerely joyous giggle.

"Perfect. Excellent. I love it."

President Monica stood up and placed her hand on the magic circle written on the wall. The circle filled with mana, and the Student Council's insignia glowed a faint white. Then she reached into the circle and plucked from it a single document. After writing something down on the piece of paper, she placed it in the envelope sitting on the table and threw it.

It didn't come flying fast like a dart or throwing star. Nor did air resistance stop it in its tracks and send it fluttering to the ground like a normal piece of paper.

The letter gently glided through the air and landed in Gabby's hand.

"But...I have one condition."

Gabby tensed.

"You must swear to surpass Benito at some point. I don't even care if it happens a while after you graduate, either. Make sure you overtake him. You're going to serve under me, after all; I won't stand for you becoming anything less."

"Why, absolutely!"

President Monica roared with laughter.

"Then let us grow stronger together."

After another moment of laughter, Monica turned her gaze to me.

"Sorry, Yuika. We've already admitted your brother into the Student Council, so I'm afraid we don't have any room left for you... *Pfft*, I'm kidding, sorry. I just wanted to try saying that. I get it. You aren't planning on joining, are you?"

She was right on the mark.

"The honor to be considered as a member of the Student Council is far more than I deserve. However, I must respectfully decline. I cannot join you."

"Well, which one will you choose, then?"

I gazed at Takioto. He stared back at me.

I got the sense that the president had already guessed which one I was going for.

"I've watched Shion for a while, so believe me, I know. That girl acts like she's above it all, but she's had to go through some harsh, trying stuff. Are you prepared to go through the same thing?"

"Of course."

"You do realize you'll be in opposition to your brother since he's in the Student Council?"

"All the more reason to join," I was able to reply. When I made my resolve clear to the president, she grinned.

"I wanted you to join the Student Council along with Gabriella, too. Honestly, we've got nothing but excellence this year."

Takioto had an errand to take care of, so he went off somewhere with Nanami. Exiting the Student Council room, Gabby and I stared at each other.

"I never once would have thought I would be talking with you like this someday."

"Same for me. You're so impulsive and quick to overreact…"

"That's quite enough, thank you very much."

Surprisingly, those might have been her best qualities.

"Will you be all right on your own?" I asked.

"*Oh-ho-ho-ho!* And just who do you think I am? This will be nothing for *moi*!"

Gabby put her hand up next to her face and chortled. Given how she looked now, she was probably going to be fine.

"Yeaaaah, I figured. Well then…let's go."

"Indeed. I'll be quite all right, but you better be careful yourself now."

We had both set out on our own paths after much deliberation. I was sure we'd eventually have some regrets. But every choice you made fore-closed certain possibilities.

From an unlimited number of options, as Takioto put it, we had chosen the ones that would bring us the least regrets.

Gabby was practically a different person now. Her face was cheerful and refreshed; it was as if her demons had been exorcised.

We both exchanged smiles. The two of us laughed.

"You have quite a pretty face right now. It's like you've grown into your womanhood."

"*Hee-hee*, but of course. And while it may not hold a candle to my own, you have lovely features yourself."

"Excuuuse me? My face is muuuch cuter than yours."

Despite my response, we didn't suddenly devolve into bickering. Instead, we simply both burst into heartfelt laughter.

Before all this, those words alone would have been enough to make us erupt in a shouting match. But now we both understood that these were just jokes. Though I did wonder how much of that Gabby was kidding about. Either way, that was fine with me. At this point, even that part of her seemed kind of adorable.

After a moment of laughter, a silence fell between us. It wasn't a bad one, though. It was a sort of embarrassing silence, the kind that made you feel antsy and itchy.

"Yuika Hijiri."

"What is it?"

"You're my close friend."

"Fine by me. I'd feel sorry for you otherwise, so I'll go ahead and accept it."

Gabby laughed at my banter. Then her mood shifted slightly, though she still wore a smile.

"But…we're going to be enemies from now on."

Gabby in the Student Council. Me in the Ceremonial Committee.

I would be up against my brother, and Gabby would be up against hers.

And we would be opposing each other, too.

"Aren't we just going back to how we were before?"

"But neither of us are the same as we once were."

She had a point there. Gabby recognized me, I recognized her, and a

kind of bond had formed between us. Even if we appeared to be quarreling with each other on the surface, this connection of ours wouldn't
disappear.

I thrust my fist out toward Gabby.

"I don't want to hear any whining now. I don't want to have to come
and chew you out over and over again."

At this, Gabby stuck her own fist out toward me and tapped it against
mine.

"I should be the one saying that to you, no? Well…when the time
comes, I'll be sure to come and laugh at you."

The two of us understood each other, acknowledged each other. From
here on out, we would play the role of enemies.

"All right then, I'll see ya later."

"I ought to be on my way as well."

We each began walking down our separate paths.

At the end of my road was my brother.

"Sorry for the holdup."

"Don't worry, I wasn't waiting at all."

Iori patted the spot next to him on the bench. I took a seat. As soon
as I did, he held out a bottle of milk tea for me. He must have bought
it ahead of time. Except it was ridiculously sweet, just like he preferred.
Not that I really cared.

"Thanks."

I opened the bottle, and an intense sweetness filled my whole mouth.
My brother had been drinking this after he had finished exercising, and
I honestly couldn't believe he could stomach it. His sweat must have
tasted like sugar.

"Well, what's up? You wanted to tell me something?"

I thought about where to begin, when suddenly, Gabby's face came
to my mind.

"…I just made a new friend."

"Oh, really? What're they like?"

"She's got drills on her head, she rushes in headlong like a run-
away machine, and she's not very considerate…but she's got her good
points, too."

"Uh, you're really laying into her here… You said she was your *friend*, right?"

"It's fine, it's all true anyway. The thing is, she took a really big step forward today."

To resolve the issues she had long kept inside her. To leap out to a new world.

I continued. "And that made me think some things over myself, too! And well, it occurred to me that you've had something on your mind lately, haven't you?"

"Yeah."

"Can you tell me why?"

"…………"

"Is it because of what happened to me?"

My brother forced a smile. Geez, he was so easy to read. That was answer enough.

It was exactly as Takioto said. It got on my nerves that he was always protecting me. I really needed to step up and look out for myself. And on top of that…

"I lost when we last fought, didn't I?"

"Yup, I won."

It had been my first defeat. It felt like there was this huge wall in front of me, and I had thought that I probably wouldn't be able to beat him again. The speed of my brother's growth was abnormal.

But Takioto had insisted that I wouldn't lose to him. He said I could beat him. Then in true Takioto fashion, he tacked on, *"Well, you won't be able to beat me, though,"* or whatever on the end there.

My brother wasn't entirely out of my reach. Those words gave me courage.

"It's so frustrating to do nothing but lose. I can't stand it."

My statement prompted my brother to laugh.

"Pfft. Heh-heh."

"What?"

"Sorry, I was just thinking that's very like you."

Well, hearing him put it like that, I had to admit it did sound like something I would say.

"That doesn't matter. I'm not going to lose to you, Big Brother."

Takioto had asserted as much.

I fully plan on becoming the strongest, but the biggest wall at the end is going to be your brother, Iori Hijiri.

If I'm able to become strong enough to scale that wall, then that'd make me the strongest of all.

"Takioto told me that you're going to become the strongest of all," I said.

"Yup, sure am."

"That's impossible," I asserted.

But I found myself thinking that I wanted to climb over that wall. There wasn't really any helping it, was there? In that case…

"Because *I'm* going to end up the strongest of all."

—Benito's Perspective—

A lot's been wrapped up. There's going to be a big event soon, and when the time comes, I'm going to need your help.

I could tell from reading Takioto's message that he had done a good job with Gabriella.

Thank goodness…truly.

I'd first noticed how Gabriella was neglected before I even turned ten.

At that time, I hadn't known what neglect was, so I assumed that our parents were busy and couldn't find the time to look after her. But after I was introduced to a young girl, I realized there was something strange about our family.

The girl's eyes had shocked me. Despite their beauty, they were distorted. Even though she wore a smile on her face, the girl had stared at me with cold eyes, as if she had given up on the world.

Things were the same now, really. Stefania had been this way for a long time.

Her family occupied a unique position, and I had known about Stefania from a young age even in Leggenze because our family was the closest to the Saint's bloodline. Her existence had led me to harbor suspicions about my own family.

This was all to say, I picked up on Gabriella's neglect in her early childhood because the despair in her eyes had resembled the despair in Stefania's for a time. Everything became clear when I looked from Gabby to my parents. Thanks to that, I had been able to change, too.

The only bright spot in this situation was that the maid serving Gabriella was an upstanding individual. She had guided her down the right path, so it was fair to say the worst-case scenario had been avoided. If the maid hadn't been there, there was no telling how Gabriella would have ended up. Or how I would have ended up, for that matter.

The maid must have felt more like a parent to Gabriella than our real mother and father did.

Concerned that my sister was lonely, I acted in Gabriella's interests in our father and mother's stead. But I'd been *too* concerned about Gabriella. I'd gotten too involved.

At first, everything was fine.

Gabriella started to smile more, learned to enjoy magic, figured out how to improve herself, and became a bright and cheerful girl.

But that wasn't how she was supposed to turn out.

I knew. The Evangelistas were hiding something. They had to be up to something behind the scenes that they needed to keep secret. In all likelihood, it involved the Saint, too.

That was why I looked into it myself, though back then, I was more motivated by my interest in the Saint than anything else.

It wasn't that I was attracted to her. Rather, I was interested in the Saint because she had the same eyes as my sister. Gabriella's eyes had been filled with despair due to parental neglect, so I assumed Stefania had problems of her own.

I often would talk to her, trying desperately to get her to break into a heartfelt smile. But she ended up taking a different emotional direction than Gabby had. I was overjoyed when, perhaps from my persistence, she spoke to me in a rough tone of voice that showed her true feelings, but she continued to avoid disclosing any information about the Saint system. Even now, Stefania candidly spoke about her emotions on a regular basis, yet still refused to tell me anything about how the Saint operated. I figured she simply *couldn't* talk about it.

With this all happening, it almost felt like I had found myself another little sister.

I didn't particularly care for my family, but I intended to take over the Evangelista line when my time came. After all, I couldn't abandon my newfound little sister.

But Gabriella was different. I wanted her to escape from our family.

I didn't want her to brush up against the Pandora's box that was Leggenze and the Saint.

I needed her to become capable of doing everything on her own.

I had convinced everyone that she had talents of her own to get them to pay attention to her, yet at the same time, I had caged her. Yes, she was talented, but she was also being robbed of her potential. By the same token, I could not deny that I was partially responsible for the warped person she had become.

But at this rate, she was going to end up locked in a cage from which there was no escape—the Evangelista family of Leggenze.

In my efforts to liberate Gabriella from our parents, I had trapped her in a different cage, one that was cruel in its own right. Though the cage was unlocked, leaving it would be no simple task, as she had been stuck there for so long that the door had rusted shut.

I didn't want Gabriella to end up like me. But since I was the only one in the cage with her, the only person she could see, she'd inevitably aspired to emulate me.

I had chosen to be caged. I didn't want Gabriella to be locked in there as well. She had such big wings on her back; it would be a shame if she didn't use them to fly free.

It wasn't that I simply didn't want her to join the Ceremonial Committee. No, I wanted her to give up on the idea that she should follow in my footsteps entirely.

If in the process of thinking about her future, she had determined it was absolutely necessary for her before joining the Ceremonial Committee of her volition, then that would have been just fine. Regrettably, in her case, it had been the former.

But now, I no longer needed to worry about any of that.

"Come on in."

I answered the knock.

"Pardon me, Brother."

One glance told me everything I needed to know.

Takioto must have pulled off something incredible. He had loosened those ever so tightly bound ill feelings in her heart, the ones I had never been able to dispel.

How I wished he could do something to help my other little sister, the Saint.

I understood it would be difficult. It involved the Saint and obscured religious circumstances. I was talking about things that could ignite a war between countries.

But if he, who bore the blood of Ryuuen Hanamura, who had earned the friendship of the Tréfle princess, who had set records that seemed utterly impossible for any human to set, wasn't going to do it, then just who would guide the situation to resolution?

"Yuika came by here yesterday, did she not?"

"Ahh, yeah, Yuika told me. That she wanted to join the Ceremonial Committee. And that you weren't going to be there with us. Everyone on the Ceremonial Committee agreed to have her. But are you sure you're okay with this?" I asked Gabby.

Shion and I had deemed Yuika strong enough to join us. Though she wasn't nobility, we'd also heard that she was under the protection of the Hanamura family, which would be enough to ward off most trouble.

"Why, yes, I am perfectly fine with it."

Just what was I going to have to do to repay Takioto for this? Gabriella had changed ever since she had met him. Of course, she still looked exactly the same on the outside. Anyone else besides me might have seen her and not noticed any changes at all. But I could tell.

Since I had been watching over Gabriella for so long.

"I thought things over, regarding you, dear Brother."

"Oh, about me, huh?"

Gabriella's eyes were different now; her attitude was different. She wasn't looking at me, but *beyond* me.

I mean, she had almost the same exact light in her eyes that President Monica did. That Iori had right now, too. The look that Takioto, the cause of it all, had in his eyes. It was Gabriella's brand-new outlook.

Ahhh. I wasn't crying right now, was I?

I absolutely couldn't cry. I couldn't let her see me like that. How could I show her something like that? After all, Gabriella had such a look of resolve in her eyes. She had the sort of determination in her chest that Takioto had, heroically pushing on toward his goals, overflowing with confidence and hope.

Oh my goodness. All my memories of Gabriella started welling up in my mind.

That time when she earned full marks on a test, but Father coldly rebuffed her by saying that I got those grades like it was nothing.

That time when Gabriella showed off a new spell to Mother, only to be told that I had learned it much faster.

She had always been compared to me. By those two stonehearted adults who only ever had family affairs on their minds.

I had wanted her to remain cheery and spirited. That was why I'd ended up cutting her off from the world. I fussed over her too much. Because I wanted her to smile. Yet I had been unable to show Gabriella a path that allowed her to soar in the great open sky.

"I am my own person. I am not the Gabriella who Mother and Father wish me to be. And…"

But she had gotten out of her cage. Takioto might have pried open the rusted door himself. Maybe Yuika had grabbed her hand from the outside and pulled her out.

"…I'm not you, either, dear Brother."

But she had been the one to leave it. Right now, she was trying to take off on her own.

"You have always protected me. That is why I want to thank you. But I want to go forward without your support from now on."

Here she was, having grown up without letting her heart rot despite being neglected, and having escaped from her cage to show me a look of determination. So why—why wasn't I allowed to cry?

"I am different from you. I have different things that I'm good at, too."

No, I couldn't. She was conveying her resolve to me. All the more reason why I couldn't show her any tears.

"I respect you, my dear Brother. I think you are the greatest in the world. But I am me. I've found a different path, one that isn't chasing after you. From here on out, I will walk down that path on my own. Then one day…"

Gabriella looked hard at me. I knew exactly what she was going to say.

"…I will beat you."

What I needed to do right now was become the headwind that would help her fly higher. Like the gust that birds catch to lift their wings up into the great blue sky.

I needed to laugh and tell her this:

"*Heh-heh*, can you really best me, I wonder?"

"Why, yes, of course I can. I am going to surpass you and become greatest in the world, after all."

—Takioto's Perspective—

Yuika and Gabby had totally different tastes, incredibly different favorite foods, and completely opposite personalities. But they were very, very close. Their relationship was bumpy and uneven. But those bumps fit well against each other, and the two girls' troubles over their older brothers had brought them together.

After agonizing over their issues, they had been able to find their goals, along with their paths ahead.

The two girls thanked me. But I hadn't done much of anything. The both of them had been strong from the start. They could think through things themselves, too. They would have been able to find a way through even without me around. I'd simply given them a little push.

In the game, Yuika has three paths she can go down, while Gabby has two.

Yuika can join the Student Council, Morals Committee, or the Ceremonial Committee, and she grows stronger in any of them. But no matter which committee she joins, her ultimate goal is always Iori. Defeating him is her sole objective.

In Gabby's case, she can choose between the Ceremonial Committee and the Student Council. But if you lose the competition with her and she joins the Ceremonial Committee, Gabby heads toward her bad ending when it comes time for the Saint's event.

However, she can avoid that by becoming independent and joining the Student Council, where she's able to grow as strong as her beloved big brother and go on to play an important role in the Saint's event.

I was truly relieved that she had chosen well. I'd secretly been worried she would screw everything up with an airheaded idea of hers.

I summarized what had happened, leaving out the things I couldn't mention, and Yukine crossed her arms knowingly.

"So you're saying that Minister Benito weighed on her mind from the very beginning. She then agonized over whether she ought to chase after him or break away from him."

"Yeah, that's the gist of it."

"And ultimately, Gabby realized she's different from Minister Benito, so she decided to surpass him by taking a path of her own instead of chasing after him."

"That's the choice she made."

"...When it's all said and done, people will still have doubts about whether they went down the right path or not."

Yukine let out a small sigh. She closed her eyes, as though she was deep in thought. Maybe she was reflecting on her past.

"The grass always looks greener on the other side; that's all there is to it. That means the most important thing is making the choice you'll regret the least. If Gabby thought things over and selected that option, then it will work out."

I nodded. I couldn't have said it better myself.

"Is there anything you regret, Master?"

At Nanami's question, I nodded with exaggeration.

"Sure, plenty of stuff."

Not everything was going perfectly. If it were, then neither Ludie nor Yuika would've ever been put in danger in the first place.

"That said, I can't let myself stop now. I have to do what I can, simple as that."

I would have several heroines' bad endings waiting for me if I didn't keep moving forward. That was something I needed to avoid at all costs.

"Anemone really did a great job, huh?"

Only a few days had passed, but she had already produced the item I'd requested.

"My mind and body are fully prepared."

"...I'm not using this on you, okay, Nanami?"

"It's an item for binding angels, right? Who else are you going to use it on if not her?"

Yukine must have thought this item was for Nanami. Though to be fair, there were definitely times when she was so out of control that I *wanted* to tie her up, sure.

"You're about to find out. Let's go."

I started walking forward. The other two followed behind me.

We were going up against our most powerful foe yet this time. I certainly couldn't defeat them on my own. Even having Nanami and Yukine at my side wouldn't tilt things in our favor.

"That reminds me, Yuika told me everything, Big Bro," Nanami teased.

"Stop, don't pour salt on the wound."

After I frantically lashed out at them, insisting that "anyone would want little sisters as cute as you two" and that "it was a totally normal opinion," the result was an apathetically dour look from Yuika, while Gabby grew slightly bashful for some reason. Whatever, I didn't care anymore!

"I'd want a little sister like those two, too," Yukine said, backing me up.

Her words of encouragement sank deep into my soul. Still, why had I ended up saying something like that anyway? Maybe it was because I had already crossed a line with the magical-girl outfits.

"If you would prefer, I wouldn't mind being your maid little sister from now on."

"Don't be stupid! A maid who doesn't call me 'Master'? That'd be like sushi without the fish!"

"That's just rice, isn't it…?"

"Yukine, that's not the point here. The important part is what's to come."

"And that would be?"

"Let's head into the library."

"Now that I think about it…I've almost never been here, have I?" Nanami remarked.

Well, of course she hadn't. I had purposely made Nanami avoid the place.

"You'll understand why once we get there."

I had brought Yukine along with me as some insurance. I was sure nothing was going to happen, but just in case, right?

Normally, she'd be working right now, so it would've taken a ton of time to find her in this huge library. However, I had already made an appointment with her, so locating Ms. Sakura was easy.

"Hello, Ms. Sakura."

"I've been waiting for you, Taki… Huh?"

She looked at Nanami and froze.

"It can't be…"

Nanami looked at her and stiffened.

The maid's petrification quickly dissipated. She took out her bow and nocked her arrow so quickly that it was as if she had detected a monster of some kind.

"Run, Master!"

"Nanami, just calm down."

"What's wrong, you two?"

But Yukine's words didn't have an effect on Nanami, as she stood with her bow ready, glaring at Ms. Sakura. Mana was flowing from her hands, and sweat was beading on her forehead.

"Here at school? Why? Did Marino know? No, of course she knew. That woman doesn't think twice about doing this sort of thing."

"Lovely weather we're having," I said, purposely ignoring the tension.

"Y-yes. Quite," Ms. Sakura replied, still unsettled. Then while keeping her eyes locked on Nanami, she asked the biggest question on her mind:

"Hey, Takioto, why…is there an angel here…?"

She must have calmed down a little, because her agitation disappeared, and her usual smile returned to her face. However, I could say for certain her eyes were not smiling; their trademark gentleness had been replaced with a piercing glare.

Ms. Sakura had instantly detected that Nanami was an angel. There was almost no one who had been able to sense Nanami's race outright, yet it had been instantaneous for this woman.

Nanami realized it the moment she saw Ms. Sakura, too. It had been a long while since I had seen the typically calm, cool, and collected maid as agitated as she was now.

"You must have known, right, Master?"

Oh yeah, of course I did. I trusted Nanami to understand that I had met with Ms. Sakura so many times while she had yet to meet her once because I didn't want to risk moving events forward.

"That silly toy Miss Anemone made isn't going to do anything against a monster like this, you know."

"Yeah, I know."

I knew, all right. Ms. Sakura's strength was on a whole other plane of existence. I understood a half-baked item wasn't going to have any effect on her. But a whole lotta things can change between having something and not, trust me.

"Hold on a sec, Takioto. What's going on here?" Yukine asked.

"I'll have to fill you in on the details a bit later."

Sorry, Yukine, but I wanted to have you along as my bodyguard just in case something happened today.

"Master, a question," Nanami said before staring hard at Ms. Sakura.

Sweat was running down the maid's cheeks, as if she was sitting inside a sauna.

"*Haaah, haah*...why, why is there... an angel in a place like this?"

Yukine was startled by the word *angel* and looked at Ms. Sakura.

She immediately put a hand on her naginata, but...

"Yukine, it's okay," I said.

She held back from readying her weapon. However, she still left a hand on the shaft, just in case.

"Nanami, there's nothing wrong with one being here, right? There are angels all over the world, living normal lives."

When I glanced over at Ms. Sakura, she nodded.

"There are, but not very many."

"Then let me ask a different question. Why is an *upper-rank* angel here?"

"Upper rank? Oh, listen to you... ♪"

Ms. Sakura didn't refute Nanami's claim and replied in a pleased tone. Nanami's gaze, however, was ice-cold.

"Then...why is an angel nearly expelled from heaven—"

Nanami said, as if she was criticizing Ms. Sakura's very existence.

"—in a place like this?!"

The atmosphere changed the instant those words left her mouth.

"*Gah!*"

Yukine let out a startled shout. It was only natural. The ground quaked, our field of view grew hazy, and simply breathing became difficult.

This wasn't because of a spell Ms. Sakura had cast.

She was simply releasing her mana. With just a twist of her pinky finger, she was able to have this much of an effect on me, Nanami, and Yukine, too.

"…I haven't even felt this much power from President Monica before. It's on par with an instructor— No, beyond even that…"

However, Ms. Sakura only smiled.

"What exactly are you plotting?!"

"Whoa, whoa, Nanami. It's okay."

I reined Nanami in.

To anyone watching, I probably looked really lame. I put on a composed front with my words, but my legs had been trembling for a while now, and there was a deluge of sweat underneath my clothes. It made me question if simply standing here was shortening my life span.

"…Kousuke Takioto was irregular from the very start, of course, but I never expected it to come to this," Ms. Sakura said, closing her eyes and getting ready to do something. But I put the brakes on this, too.

"Now, now, Ms. Sakura, you're getting a bit hasty here. C'mon, let's just relax, get nice and calm."

Ms. Sakura slowly opened her eyes and stared hard at me. Was I looking into the eyes of a dragon here or something?

I let out a tiny sigh to compose myself. Then I slowly begin releasing my own mana.

"Oh, so you know what I was trying to do?"

"But of course, Ms. Sakura. If I were in your position, I probably would have made the same move myself."

To avoid the worst possible scenario, she may not have had any other choice. However, I wasn't going to allow it.

"Ms. Sakura, you and I are pretty much different in every way, but there is one thing that we both have in common. Did you know that?"

"…And what would that be, I wonder?"

I continued releasing my magic, as if I was confronting the librarian.

"You're beautiful, a skilled magic-user, a high-ranking angel, and a very kind person, so at first glance, we may not seem anything alike."

"Master, you're very handsome."

"You're sweet, Takioto."

The two angels still had their guards up, but their jokes showed they had grown more accustomed to the mana around them.

"Please, Takioto, hearing you bare your feelings like that while your girlfriends are standing right there—you're embarrassing me."

She didn't look embarrassed whatsoever to me. That wasn't the point. I had to get back on topic.

"See, the thing with me?" I said, closing my eyes. Then I remembered.

"I like this world."

I thought back to the first time I'd used magic, the first time I went into a dungeon. The moment I'd met Marino, Sis, Ludie, and Claris, when I saw Yukine for the first time, when I encountered Nanami, when I went with Yuika and Gabby on our dungeon trip together... When I'd first gone to school. Iori, Katorina, Orange, President Monica, Shion, Saint Stef, Vice President Fran, Minister Benito... The people, the city, the dungeons... I loved it all.

"You like this world, too, don't you, Ms. Sakura? You wouldn't be doing something like this if you didn't."

"......"

"Please answer me. Do you like it or dislike it? That's all I ask."

That would help me make up my mind.

"I like it, yes. I love it."

Ahhh. Just hearing her say that was more than enough. I released even more and more of my mana.

My mind was set, and the shaking in my legs disappeared. I stuck out my chest more so that this terrifying monster wouldn't underestimate me.

"Thank goodness. In that case, can you wait a bit longer, just a little bit longer? I'll finalize preparations, and then Iori will come to you."

"Yes, I'm sure he will."

"Then you're going to use Iori when he does come to you."

Iori hadn't fully completed the event. He needed to wait just a bit longer to learn about Ms. Sakura. Until that time came, I didn't want to advance this event any further.

"Once Iori comes here, use him however you want, but can you wait a little while?"

Ms. Sakura's event left regrets for many people on their first playthrough. A great many eroge players had shed tears in front of their monitors.

"Do I stand to gain anything from doing that?"

"*Ha-ha*, sure you do. A lot to gain."

I had done the exact same thing while watching the scene. Seeing the all-too-cruel circumstances, the choice that she made, I couldn't get the tears to stop.

I absolutely had to prevent that from happening.

"I'm going to show you a world that your prophecies could never show you."

"...*You* will? Impossible."

I wasn't after any bad endings or any normal endings.

"I sure can."

I was after a happy ending.

I had sought strength and gotten this far in order to save you, Ms. Sakura, to save everybody. I was going to push forward doing exactly that, too. I couldn't afford to stumble here.

All right, now was the time to spread out my stole and release as much mana as possible with a smile.

I faced the archangel, her overwhelming power far eclipsing both President Monica and Yukine, and made my declaration.

"After all...I'm the guy who's even going to surpass you and become the strongest of them all."

Hello there. Iris here, I'm alive.

—Acknowledgments—

To Noboru Kannatuki, thank you as always for your wonderful illustrations. Between your dark-elf character design and Gabby dripping wet, they were absolutely amazing. Your illustration of Gabby on the cover especially brought out her wonderful charms!

Thank you to Yukari Higa for your manga adaptation. The release bonuses you made were especially fantastic. If any of you still haven't picked it up…please do!

Oryou, thank you for your Hatsumi illustration. You're the person I always think of when it comes to illustrations of mature, older sister characters, and I was truly overjoyed to have an artist like you draw her.

To my editor Miyakawa, allow me to bow my forehead to the floor and give you my deepest gratitude. It is because of your work that this series is able to continue, and for that, I thank you.

Thank you very much to Acerola for collaborating on the latest promotional video. I have your company to thank for the wonderful video we came up with. When I was still young, there was a time I dreamed of being a game designer, and this video allowed me to live that dream a little bit. You can purchase Acerola's games at any of the major indie-game marketplaces. I encourage any who are interested to pick them up! ※They are all 18+, however.

Ludie really lets her hair
down in the Hanamura house

(Noboru Kannatuki)